ALAN JUDD

SLIPSTREAM

SIMON &
SCHUSTER

London · New York · Sydney · Toronto · New Delhi

A CBS COMPANY

First published as *Out of the Blue* in Great Britain
by Simon & Schuster UK Ltd, 2015
A CBS COMPANY
This paperback edition published 2016

Copyright © Alan Judd 2015

1 3 5 7 9 10 8 6 4 2

Simon & Schuster UK Ltd
1st Floor
222 Gray's Inn Road
London WC1X 8HB

www.simonandschuster.co.uk

Simon & Schuster Australia, Sydney
Simon & Schuster India, New Delhi

A CIP catalogue record for this book is available
from the British Library

Paperback ISBN: 978-1-4711-5604-5
eBook ISBN: 978-1-47115-063-0

This book is a work of fiction. Names
the author's imagination or are used fictitiously. Any resemblance
to ... living or dead, events or locales
is entirely coincidental.

To Nigel, Susan and Stephen Judd

Chapter One

Frank Foucham winced at the flash of light. It was only the afternoon sun catching the stream where he had cast his fly but he couldn't help it. Nor could he stop the trembling in his arms that followed. His hands were not obviously shaking but the tiny rapid quivering of his muscles was enough to vibrate the tip of his rod. He lowered it into the long grass and clasped his hands hard. The shakes came only now and again but if Phil, the squadron doctor, saw him spill his beer in the mess he might take him off flying.

He kept his eyes on his fly, which was still on the water. It was an Infallible, a wet fly, which meant that it would gradually sink. He would have preferred a dry fly, or at least some grease to keep his line afloat, but there was no chance of finding either. He had been a keen angler since his first boyhood trips with his stepfather, back home in Canada, but now, here in wartime England, he no longer minded whether he caught anything. You were almost never alone in the air force and he treasured these rare periods of solitude, content to be in the presence of the unknown, loving the quiet mystery of dark pools as much as – perhaps more than – solving it.

The flash of sun on water recalled others he had seen that morning, distant flashes from the greenhouses and windows of northern France 15,000 feet below. And later those other flashes, less pure white, mixed with red and yellow and sometimes a puff of black smoke, as rockets from the low-flying Typhoons found targets on the German airfield. One, a Focke-Wulf 190, was on the runway and had almost got off the ground when it burst into flames and skidded into others parked nearby. That made a bigger flash, with much more red and a great revolving pall of black smoke.

It was just after this, as Frank tipped his Spitfire left to get a better view, that he saw the other flash, the one like the flash of sun on water, very brief and pure white, on his right quarter.

At the same moment his headphones were filled by Patrick's voice. 'Foxtrot Alpha One break right!'

He heaved on the stick, banking and turning so tightly that he felt the flesh of his neck bulge and the blood begin to drain from his head. For a long second he hung vertically and seemingly motionless on the propeller, his engine roaring and straining, while the white flash mutated into the cockpit window of an FW190, closing fast. It had already opened fire, tracer rounds streaking just below him. For every one that glowed there would be nine unseen. He had a vivid glimpse of the German plane's yellow propeller spinner and the immaculate black eagle on its fuselage, then he was alone, twisting and climbing into an empty sky.

It was anything but, of course.

He looped upside down out of his turn to see below him a mêlée of Focke-Wulfs and Spitfires wheeling, soaring and plummeting above the spiralling smoke from burning aircraft and camouflaged corrugated hangars on the airfield below. The remaining Typhoons, their job done, headed low and fast for home, pursued by the black puffs of exploding anti-aircraft shells, leaving several of their squadron burning fiercely in the woods.

The Focke-Wulf did not pursue Frank through his upward spiral, knowing he could be out-turned by Spitfires and trusting to his superior acceleration to get away. He had judged well; by the time Frank saw him again he was out of range and climbing like a demented bee. Frank gave him a burst, half in acknowledgement, half as a sop to his own pride. If it hadn't been for Patrick's call the German would have had him, deservedly.

Below Frank the scrap was in full spate, the sky now teeming with Focke-Wulfs where there had been none moments before. The British attack had achieved surprise, with the Typhoons going in below the tree-tops, and it was unlikely that any Germans had got off the ground. The Focke-Wulfs were probably from Évreux-Fauville, a formidable lot only a few minutes' flying time away. Frank's face was hot, his palms sweating, the muscles in his arms trembling. He broke left and tipped his wings to get a better view. A Spitfire flashed across his nose, the pilot's goggled face turned towards him in horrified surprise. Shaken by the Spitfire's slipstream, he heaved on the stick and banked left again. Three thousand feet below he saw the Dodger in Foxtrot Alpha Four chasing a smoking Focke-Wulf as it dived to get away. Unable to close but still within range, the Dodger was firing short bursts, clinical, controlled, concentrating on his kill. Concentrating too well; behind and above him, gaining fast, were two more Focke-Wulfs. Don't chase the damaged down, Patrick was always telling them, look out for your own tail.

Frank put his nose down and opened the throttle, shouting 'Alpha Four break now, break now!' into his radio. Alpha One vibrated as she always did in a dive, not dangerously, but as if quivering with excitement. He closed on the nearer Focke-Wulf's rear quarter at over 400 knots, adjusted his sights, counted three more seconds and pressed the trigger. At that moment the Dodger broke right and climbed steeply, either spotting his pursuers or in response to Frank's call. The Focke-Wulf did the same and Frank's cannon shells passed inches below its tail-plane. But the farther Focke-Wulf made the same mistake as his quarry, concentrating too hard and breaking right to pursue the Dodger. As he turned, he briefly filled Frank's sights, two white plumes trailing his clipped wingtips, his markings clear.

Bits flew off him as Frank's cannon shells struck behind the cockpit. There was no burst of flame or smoke but the entire aircraft shuddered as if in an unsteady camera frame, then began an almost leisurely roll to the right, nose down, showing its yellow underbelly. Frank steepened his dive and gave it a long burst, his shells exploding into the fuselage. As he broke away it went into a spin and the cockpit cover flew off. For an instant he could see the pilot struggling to get out. He would have no chance.

Frank levelled out at under 3000 feet. He was over woods and fields, miles from the airfield, with no other planes now visible save for the last moments of the plummeting Focke-Wulf, spinning and smoking. It hit the ground with a wide flash and a plume of thick black smoke. Frank began a long, turning climb, watching for anything behind or above. His hands were clammy and sweat trickled down inside his goggles. A tremor in his legs made him feel he wanted to kick out or get up and run around. It was sickening to see a fellow pilot, even a German one, atomised in an instant of heat. But there was also the elation that always followed a kill, the thrill of victory in mortal combat, the sense of potency. It was like being back at school and scoring a goal, only here you were on your own with no one to cheer you, just that coiling black smoke to mark an extinction that could have been you.

At 10,000 feet he circled, looking for the target airfield. It was marked by flames and smoke miles to the north now, with just two or three dark specks circling above like distant crows. Huns, probably, since the scrap was over. The Spits must have been low on fuel and Patrick would have told them to break for home. Frank was Patrick's wingman and they'd be wondering what had happened to him. He had enough fuel to get home provided he didn't run into trouble. It was always dangerous, returning without a wingman. The enemy, thoroughly aroused by the poking of their nest, would be hunting in pairs for returning marauders, especially damaged ones. Frank checked all his systems. He was undamaged, but still vulnerable. There was broken cloud at 20,000 feet, not much, but any cover was better than none.

Forty gallons meant he had enough fuel to gain height. He resumed his climb, heading west in order to give the airfield a wide berth before setting course 323 degrees for home. Foxtrot Alpha One's Merlin engine note was reassuringly steady. Frank loved his aeroplane.

Chapter Two

Frank taxied to Dispersal, revved the engine to clear it, then switched everything off and sat motionless, savouring the silence before the ground crew clambered up around him. His head still rang with noise and vibration and he could smell the hot fumes, but for half a minute the healing balm of silence spread from within, like consciousness of grace. Even the shouts and exclamations of the mechanics, startlingly clear after the distortions of the radio, did not at first dispel it.

He had picked up the Dodger on the way back, finding him limping along at 230 knots and 15,000 feet, a tell-tale thin dark vapour-line of burnt oil behind. Frank was at 20,000 feet and just within sight of the coast of France. He approached the Dodger in a long shallow dive, well off to his right so as not to alarm him. When he was parallel and sure of being seen and identified, he moved in close. There were no flames but the Dodger's engine cowling was streaked with oil and holed near the rear. He flew level, however, and his prop was regular. Not wanting to give their position away by breaking radio silence, Frank tipped his wings and held up his thumb, wriggling it from vertical to horizontal. The Dodger's goggled face grinned and he held his thumb up. Frank dropped back and climbed to 17,000 feet, playing guardian angel all the way back to the Kent coast. By the time they reached the airfield the Dodger's oil vapour was thickening ominously and he was feathering his engine. He turned it off and glided down to a perfect landing.

Roused by the ground crew, Frank unharnessed himself and pushed back his cockpit canopy. For a few seconds more he still carried the silence within him, like a full glass of water. Always, even after a successful mission with reason to celebrate – another kill – he was reluctant to re-engage, to spill the water. And always, the moment the glass was smashed, he thought no more of it.

A tractor was towing the Dodger's plane off the end of the runway, fire engine and ambulance in attendance. Frank could just make out the Dodger's squat shape and characteristic gesticulations. Uninjured, evidently. That was no surprise; it was possible to imagine the Dodger not existing at all but impossible to imagine a lesser, maimed or disabled Dodger. It seemed his body could barely contain his energy. Like him or loathe him, he filled a room, was a quick and adept pilot, daring in combat to the point of foolhardiness, impulsive and unpredictable. He owed his nickname to his ability to dodge trouble both in the air and on the station, where he often sailed pretty close to the wind. Frank envied him his confidence and was pleased to have been able to shepherd him home.

In the debrief afterwards the Dodger was exuberant. 'Did you get him? Did you get the bastard who got me?'

'I got him. The film will confirm. But I got him.'

The Dodger slapped him on the shoulder, his grin showing nearly all his large, widely spaced teeth.

'Good old Moose. First I knew of it was a bloody great bang and I could see bugger all, oil all over my goggles, half my instruments gone. Talk about flying blind, all I could do was heave up and away till the fog cleared. Marvel I didn't fly into anyone. Christ knows what happened to the bastard I was chasing. Sure I hit him. Did anyone see?'

Tim, the lanky Kiwi, thought he might have seen him go down but couldn't be sure. Nor was anyone else. The squadron hadn't lost anyone and had accounted for two Focke-Wulfs, including Frank's, plus a possible, so the atmosphere was cheerful. The Typhoons had suffered badly, though, losing two to flak, another to the Focke-Wulfs and a fourth caught by the explosion of the third. It was too often the way with low-level attacks on defended targets: they might work but they were always costly. Someone thought another Typhoon had fallen prey to two Focke-Wulfs near the end of the scrap but someone else reckoned he had intercepted them, allowing it to escape. An argument began.

Patrick held up his hand. 'Cut it. Leave it to film and body count. We'll find out later.' There was immediate silence. They sat on their fold-up chairs, looking at him. He was seated at the table with the station intelligence officer. The wing commander was elsewhere. 'Now, before you all cut along for nosh, one more thing.' He lit another cigarette, taking his time. Patrick never hurried, never raised his voice, never needed to. He spoke with a calm assurance that was assumed by those with no experience of it to be due to his Eton schooling. He missed nothing and pulled no punches, but was never less than polite. 'We nearly lost two pilots today through basic errors, errors you all know to avoid. Dodger, because you were too intent on your prey even after he was obviously hit and out of it. You didn't look behind you. It's basic, elementary. You'd have hit the ground before he did – if he did – if Frank hadn't saved your bacon. And Frank, right at the start because you were hanging around sight-seeing, looking at the pretty pictures on the ground instead of looking out for Jerry. You should have seen those 190s before I did. They came from your side and damn nearly caught us all napping. Save daydreaming for your fishing and keep your eyes peeled, all the time. That applies to everyone.' He looked at the young faces around him, silent and solemn now. 'Apart from that, well done everybody. It was a good score and we gave the Typhoons time to do a proper job on the airfield, which they did, poor buggers. A good show. Well done.'

There was bacon and eggs in the mess, smelling better than it looked or tasted. The Dodger sat next to Frank, held up his single thin rasher and snorted like a pig. 'You saved mine. Guess you're entitled to this.' His Mancunian voice carried along the table, prompting dismissive remarks about the bacon.

'Keep it on account,' said Frank. 'Save mine next time.'

The Dodger held his rasher up to the light. 'So bloody thin it's transparent, look. Like fag paper. Rizla Red, that's all it is.'

Afterwards, the Dodger, Tim and a couple of others remained at the table and resumed their analysis of the scrap. Frank took his tea over to the armchairs, where Patrick was reading a paper. 'I should have given you my bacon,' he said. He so respected Patrick, so wanted to please him, that he was often nervous about speaking to him. 'You saved mine.'

Patrick shook his head and proffered his cigarettes. 'You'll do the same for me.'

'Sorry that I—'

Don't be.' He held up his lighter for Frank. 'Why don't you push off for the rest of the day? Go fishing. You like fishing, don't you? No more ops planned. We're stood down. The other lot are on standby. Take Roddy's bike.'

Roddy had gone down during a scrap over Calais a few days before, spinning helplessly with half his port wing shot away. His possessions had been cleared from their hut with the usual prompt and discreet efficiency but his bike was still outside.

'Have it,' continued Patrick, 'have it as yours. It wasn't really his, anyway. He inherited from Ian. Or maybe what's-his-name – Bruce, the South African. Before your time, anyway.' He exhaled forcefully. 'Not that there's much for a fly-fisher here in Kent, is there?'

'A few. Brown trout. Nothing big but just enough for a bit of sport.'

'We should move the squadron to Hampshire. You'd have the Avon, then. Mainly coarse fish but there are some decent trout to be had on mayfly. Even a few salmon below Fordingbridge. Better still the Test, of course. Beautiful river, the most perfect chalk stream.'

Patrick's range of accomplishments never ceased to surprise. He had learned to fly at Oxford, won a blue as a half-miler and seemed to know a bevy of senior generals, admirals and air marshals.

'I didn't know you fished.'

'Used to. Get back to it one day. Can't think of anything better than a day on the Test, right now.' Patrick yawned. 'Well done this morning, anyway.'

'Sorry again about the sight-seeing.'

'We all do it. Need each other to remind ourselves. It'll be me next time. Just make sure you tell me. Go and catch a fish.'

On his way out of the mess Frank saw a letter from his mother on the round table in the entrance, obvious immediately by its Canadian stamp and her hand. It was a short account of home, the farm, his father, his brothers and sisters, the puppy he hadn't seen, nothing of herself and at the end a brief but telling wish that all was well with him. It was clear she hadn't got his last, sent some time – weeks, perhaps, he had lost track – ago. Her restraint was eloquent of her concern and reproach. He pushed the letter into his tunic pocket, intending to reply that evening. He would fish first.

Chapter Three

Roddy's bike was an ancient black Hercules, heavy-framed with pitted handlebars, three-speed gears, no lights and a warped leather saddle. The tyres were pumped up. Frank remembered Roddy on it, pedalling slowly, his blond head bent low over the handlebars. He was a quiet man, an equable Londoner, always carrying a book. Frank had no idea where he went on his bike, apart from using it to get around the airfield. Perhaps he rode off into the country to read, seeking silence, like Frank. He'd joined the squadron a week or so before Frank and had lasted about six, therefore. They hadn't spoken more than half a dozen times.

When Frank mounted the bike, his tackle slung in a kitbag over his shoulder and his rod tied to the crossbar with string from the station office, he discovered why Roddy used to ride so slowly and with such apparent effort. It was stuck in top gear and no amount of fiddling with the cable would move it. The rear wheel would have to come off and the hub be dismantled. He would put up with it for now and do that another time, as Roddy had no doubt intended. And perhaps Bruce before him, and whoever it was before Bruce. No one really owned anything on the airfield; if you used something regularly you acquired a temporary and informal title to it, until you were gone. Best known and most coveted was what was known as Martin's motorbike, a much-abused BSA 250cc whose temporary owner was anyone who could be bothered to tinker with it enough to keep it going. No one now remembered who Martin had been.

It was not far to the Beult, the nearest fishable stream, and Frank enjoyed his meditative progress through the elm-lined lanes of Kent, a welcome change from flying at 300 knots a few feet above them. The Beult, a small stream, was low that summer. He had already fished the most accessible reaches, with ready permission from the landowners who were pleased to indulge a pilot. But with the water now so low, there was only one stretch that would do, a slow bend with deeper pools shaded by willows, hidden from the lane by an orchard. Unable to discover the landowner, he had fished it several times without permission.

He hid his bike behind the hedge by the humped

stone bridge and set off through the orchard. They were old trees, high and awkwardly angled, full of young apples that would be difficult to pick. In a month or two there would be pickers, ladders, baskets and busy-ness, and after them the hop-pickers for the hopping, but now there was no sound apart from the regular soft brush of his boots in the grass and the hum of insects. No birdsong, no aircraft. It was mid-afternoon, warm but not hot, and the fish would probably not be feeding. But he wouldn't mind that, or not very much. The point was to be there. It was enough that the world seemed peaceful and somnolent.

A gate in the hedge on the far side of the orchard opened into a field of cow-pats and flattened grass. There were no cows, unless they were behind the willows and alders at the bend of the stream. He chose a pool he had fished before, hidden from view by long grass but with sufficient gap between the trees for him to cast.

Half an hour after the white flash and still fish-less, he had not moved on. The trembling in his arms had stopped and he was no longer troubled by images of all those earlier flashes. As the afternoon cooled into evening the trout might rouse themselves to feed. Anyway, it was good to feel hidden and private, a time to recollect himself. He cast again and watched his fly slowly sink until soft sounds of champing and swishing announced a dozen reddish-brown and white cows in a semi-circle behind him. Some were twisting and tearing the grass with their long tongues but most stared at him, dark eyes passively curious, tails swinging.

A while after that the gentle champing stopped. He looked round to see that the cattle had moved farther from the bank and were grouped more closely, facing the orchard. A tall man in a tweed suit and deer-stalker was closing the gate. Frank's first thoughts were that he looked like a traditional landowner who would not be welcoming then that he must be hot in that suit. Frank turned back to the stream, pretending to concentrate on his line. If the man kept to the field rather than the riverbank he might not see the poacher, but after a minute or two Frank heard footsteps in the grass. There was no point in further pretence, so he turned. The man seemed a walking incarnation of pepper-and-salt, in the pattern of his tweeds, his hair, his mottled white moustache and even the stippled bark of the thumbstick he leant upon when he stopped. He looked old to Frank, at least of uncertain age, his red complexion wrinkled like parchment, his eyes blue and bloodshot.

Frank began winding in his line. 'I'm sorry, sir, I guess I shouldn't be here.'

'Indeed you should not.' The voice was deep. If it had a colour it would have been walnut.

'Don't worry, I'm on my way.'

The man held up a hand and shook his head. His drooping cheeks wobbled like a bloodhound's. 'Carry on, carry on. Join you if I may.' He sat stiffly on the bank a couple of yards from Frank, sighing with the effort. He took off his deerstalker, revealing more of his white hair peppered with flecks of brown, and fumbled in his jacket pocket.

Frank paused in his winding. 'If you're sure that's OK. Kind of you, sir.'

'My river, your fish, if you get any. Which I doubt.' He took out a curved pipe and began filling it from a leather pouch as wrinkled as his face. 'What's that fly you're using?'

'An Infallible, it's the only—'

The man wobbled his cheeks again. 'You need a dry fly on this stream.'

'Haven't got any. Nor any oil for the line.'

'Wet flies never do on the Beult.'

Frank resisted the temptation to say he'd done pretty well with them so far. 'You fish a lot, sir?'

'Not now.' The man lit his pipe. 'Unless you're going to tell me you've had luck with wet fly here before?'

Frank smiled. ''Fraid I have, sir. Sorry for that.'

The man smiled, too, showing a full set of discoloured teeth. He flicked his match into the stream.

'What rod is that?'

'It's an American rod, it's a—'

19

'Are you?'

Frank explained. He had it off pat now: the family farm north of Toronto, aeronautical engineering at university, his decision to interrupt his studies and join the RAF before the war ended. 'Guess I didn't have to hurry much after all. I missed the Battle of Britain but that's about it. Doesn't look like the war's ending any time soon.' In fact, it did; or at least the beginning of the end. Preparations for the landings, the second front, would have been as obvious to the landowner as to him. Everyone was aware of the influx of troops, guns and armour into south-eastern counties, the restrictions on travel and movement in coastal areas, but no one was supposed to discuss what they were for.

'Where north of Toronto?' asked the man.

'Well, the area's called Algonquin. It's not near anywhere really. Lot of lakes.'

The man nodded.

'You know it?' If he did, he would be the first Frank had met in England.

'Heard of it.' He tamped and relit his pipe. 'You need to drop your fly nearer the bank. They get in underneath it.'

Frank doubted that. The water there was shallower and faster, with less food, but it was politic to show willing. He didn't need to re-cast but simply lifted the fly out and dropped it in nearer the bank where the current was rapid, too rapid for any fish to linger. He was beginning to resent the owner's interest. He wanted to be alone, to float like the dry fly he did not have, unburdened by conversation, his mind drifting on silence.

'Closer in, as close to the bank as you can get it. The water's slower there.'

Frank obediently flicked the fly out and dropped it farther upstream, inches from the bank, the tip of his rod just brushing the grass. Another ten or twenty minutes and, with luck, the man would get bored and go away. When the fish bit he was almost too slow with his strike. It was a brown trout, less than a pound, but spirited enough to put up a fight.

'Give it to me.' The man held out his hand. Frank landed it, extracted the fly and handed the slippery, wriggling thing to its owner who despatched it with a crisp knock on the head with the bowl of his pipe. 'Same place again. Bound to be another.'

Within less than five minutes there was a pair lying on the grass between them, silvered and stippled, as streamlined as a Spitfire's fuselage. After a few more minutes of silence the man pocketed his pipe and got stiffly to his feet. He picked up the fish and wrapped them in dock leaves.

'Come and eat them. About seven. They'll be nicely done then, with spinach and potatoes from the garden. Nothing special.'

'Well, that's kind of you, sir.' Frank normally gave anything he caught to the mess cook, with whom he secretly ate it in the kitchen. It would be a treat to eat out. 'Where do I come?'

'Carry on over the bridge and down the lane for about half a mile. Take the first right towards the village – no signposts now, of course, but there's a large oak on the corner. Then it's the first house you come to, just before the church, set back from the road, behind some trees. Called the Manor but the sign's not easy to see.'

Frank fished for another forty-five minutes, with no result. The sun was touching the tops of the elms as he packed up and walked through the munching cattle to his bike. There was no need to warn the mess he wouldn't be there for dinner – they never knew how many or how few they might have to cater for – and there was no particular time by which he had to be back, so long as he was ready for ops first thing in the morning. The prospect of different people and a different conversation cheered him.

The lane narrowed after the bridge, funnelling through burgeoning cow parsley and a copse filled with the scent of wild garlic. At the turning to the village the upright of the finger-post had been left in place, with just the arms removed. He didn't know which village it was and, indeed, never reached it because the manor and church came first. The house was hidden by trees and great cumulus banks of rhododendrons but was indicated by faded white lettering on a crumbling brick gate pillar.

He surprised himself by feeling he ought to dismount at the gate, untucking his trousers from his socks. He pushed the bike up the rough drive, suspecting that if there had been a sign saying 'Tradesmen's Entrance' he might have taken it. Ironic, he thought, given that his family's farm in Canada was no doubt a considerable multiple in size of whatever the English gentleman owned.

It was a modest manor of old red brick, gabled in the Dutch style. There was a half-circle of lawn, intersected by the drive, and a wide front door at the top of three steps. The white paint on the doors and windows was fading and peeling and the brickwork needed pointing. An open lopsided wooden shed to one side showed the back of a large black car which looked as if it hadn't moved for a long time. Petrol rationing was tight for civilians, he remembered.

He leant the bike against the shed and mounted the steps. There was a rusting iron bell-pull in the wall but no knocker. The bell felt as if it hadn't been pulled for a long time and made a sound like a distant gong.

Nothing happened. After a minute or so he pulled again and had just let go when the door was opened by a young woman. She was older than him, he guessed, but still in her twenties. Her shaped dark hair just touched her shoulders. She was dressed as if to go out, in high heels, a tight black skirt and white blouse.

For a moment neither spoke. Frank realised he didn't even know the old guy's name. 'I'm sorry, I don't – my name's—'

'You must be the trout man.' Her smile was wide and quick. 'The man who's going to share them, I mean. He told me about you. Please come in.'

They were in a large panelled hall with a staircase leading off. In the middle was a round table on which books, magazines, newspapers and letters were arranged in neat piles. An old spaniel ambled over to Frank and began sniffing his trousers.

'Don't mind Tinker, he's blind.'

'I don't mind, I like dogs. I'm Frank, by the way, Frank Foucham. I'm over here with the RAF.' He felt he was speaking too fast.

'I gathered.' Her smile switched on and off again as they shook hands. 'I'm Vanessa. I'll tell the colonel you're here.'

She disappeared through one of the doors opening off the hall, her glossy high heels crisp and decisive on the parquet floor. High heels and stockings, hard to get over here now, he thought. She must be going out but where, with whom? And where was 'out' if you lived here – surely not the church or the village pub? And how did you get to 'out', wherever it was, in heels like that? You sure as hell wouldn't walk. Perhaps you got picked up in somebody's car, somebody with access to rationed petrol. Or the black market. He remained staring at the door she had closed. When she spoke it made him feel she was a generation older than him; she had one of those very clear, cut-glass English voices that sounded as if they were putting you down even when they weren't, the sort that Patrick had probably grown up with. Yet she couldn't be much older than him.

Tinker continued his devoted sniffing of Frank's trousers. He was a Springer, liver and white, obviously old and pretty overweight. From somewhere within a clock struck the half-hour. The hall smelt of furniture polish and looked clean and well-kept, unlike the outside of the house.

Another door opened and the old man appeared, minus his deerstalker. As he walked towards Frank, holding out his hand, his resemblance to Tinker was striking. 'Ovenden, Kenneth Ovenden.'

Frank introduced himself. The colonel kept hold of his hand. 'Foucham. How do you spell it?'

Frank spelt it.

'You were christened Frank, not Francis?'

'Always Frank, sir, never Francis.'

The colonel nodded and let go of his hand.

'And I understand you're Colonel Ovenden? Is that right, sir?'

'Lieutenant-colonel. One is always promoted in the vernacular. Last show, though, so nothing for you to worry about now. Call me Kenneth.'

For the rest of their short acquaintance, Frank never did. It was not a conscious decision, more an unconscious acknowledgement, recognition of an identity the colonel needed to survive.

The colonel indicated the door he had just used. 'We'll go straight in, if you don't mind. They're done, the trout. You didn't get any more?'

The dining room was also panelled but painted a faded cream. There was a polished dining table with ten or twelve ornate but rickety old chairs, also polished. Above the marble fireplace was the portrait of a woman on a garden seat with a book on her lap. Her green eyes were smiling, focused beyond the painter, and her auburn hair was pinned up in a bun from which one or two strands escaped. Her legs were crossed and her long dark skirt revealed shoes that might have been ankle-length boots. She wore a light shawl over her cream blouse and around her neck a fine gold chain and pendant. There was tension between the formal arrangement of the painting and its execution, the tones, colours and lines of the latter suggesting a life beyond the canvas that the conventional arrangement denied.

The table was laid at the fireplace end, for two. The colonel gestured to Frank to sit and took a bottle from the sideboard. 'Little low on wine but I think this should go nicely with river trout. I had hoped my cellar would last the war but now I'm not so sure.'

The cutlery was engraved, the water was in a silver jug and there were clean white napkins in silver rings. Frank had briefly assumed that Vanessa would join them but, of course, she must be going out.

The colonel poured for them both. 'What do you fly?'

They were not far into the subject when the other door opened and Vanessa entered with two plates of trout, new potatoes and spinach, her skirt and blouse protected by an unmarked white apron.

'They've shrunk a bit in the cooking, I'm afraid, but a change from rations, and the potatoes and spinach are from the garden. We've got tons of both.'

'Change from stodgy mess food, too,' said Frank. 'They'll be just fine, I'm sure.' They did indeed seem sadly diminished but they looked good and the smell was tantalising. He raised his glass. 'I'm very grateful. It's kind of you to feed a stray airman. Especially one that was caught poaching from you. Thank you.'

The colonel raised his glass in acknowledgement but his watery blue eyes were on Vanessa, who had turned to the door. 'Are you sure?' he asked.

She nodded and smiled.

'Hope you have a good evening,' ventured Frank.

'Thank you. And you.' She closed the door.

The dinner was full of flavour but Frank had to slow his eating in order not to finish too long before the colonel, who chewed very thoroughly. His questions about the qualities of British and German planes showed surprising knowledge, though he stopped just short of making Frank feel he was being pumped for information he shouldn't give.

'I gather this latest Focke-Wulf 190 will out-perform even the Spitfire XIV,' the colonel said.

'In outright speed, yes, but the Spit will out-turn it.' Frank accepted more wine. 'We're about equal in a scrap but you're right, a well-flown 190 is pretty formidable.'

'How about the Americans – Mustangs, Lightnings, Thunderbolts, that sort of thing?'

'Can't touch it.'

'And this new one of ours, the Tempest. Any good?'

'I've never flown one. Never seen one.' Frank hadn't realised that anyone outside the RAF knew of its existence. Patrick had had a test flight and rated it highly.

'Pretty good, I'm told, but hard to handle.'

'That's what I heard. You meet a lot of fliers around here, sir?'

The colonel nodded. 'They come and go.'

When eventually he had finished, which was a while before he ceased to masticate, the colonel pointed to the sideboard. 'No pudding, I'm afraid, but there's cheese, if you like cheddar.'

It was a hunk of cheddar such as Frank hadn't seen since reaching England, even in the RAF which, like the other services, was better supplied than the population at large. 'I guess rationing hits you less in the country than in the towns?'

'It does, yes, and we take full advantage of it, I fear.' The colonel's large mottled hand trembled as he cut himself a piece. It reminded Frank of his own hands, which were fine now. 'No real shortage of eggs, milk or vegetables, in season. Red meat harder to come by, of course, but we eat the chickens when they go off lay and there are no end of rabbits, fortunately. I've taken to potting the odd squirrel, too. Ever had squirrel?'

'Can't say I have, sir, no.'

'Only the greys, one of our less desirable American imports. Quite good, bit stringy. Like cat, I imagine. Think we need another bottle, don't you?' Bending slowly, he took one from the cupboard beneath the sideboard. 'Would you mind doing the honours this time? My hands. Arthritis, I suppose.'

When they were seated he looked at Frank as if he had said something remarkable. 'Foucham. Unusual name. Tell me about your family, where it came from.'

Frank described the farm, his mother's English descent, his stepfather's Scottish origins. 'Foucham is

29

my real father's name. My mother remarried after the last war. My brothers and sisters are all called McCluskey.'

'Remember your father?'

'Never saw him. He was killed near the end of the war. I was conceived before he left.'

'What was he in?'

Frank shook his head. 'It's bad of me. I should know. I've been told.'

'Any idea where?'

'I must ask my mother. Like I said, I did know. His family was French Canadian, from Quebec. His father, anyway. His mother was from England, I do know that.' He sensed he was disappointing the colonel. 'How about your own war, sir? What were you in?'

'My war?' The colonel shook his head. 'Same as most people's. Local regiment, Royal West Kents – either them or the Buffs in this part of the world – eighth battalion, a Kitchener battalion. We did the usual things in the usual places, Loos, the Somme, Ypres, Amiens. I was lucky. But you, what brought you all the way from Canada to the RAF? Why not the RCAF?'

Frank recounted his early love for all things mechanical, the special glamour of mechanical things that flew, the growing number of airstrips in Canada – they had one on their farm – and the friend of his stepfather's who would take them lake-hopping in his seaplane. Then university to study aeronautical engineering, getting his flying licence, the hours he accumulated landing more often on water than on land, finally running into some of the RAF pilots sent to train in the safety of Canada. Hearing from them about the air war in Europe and the shortage of pilots in Britain made him determined to get there. He met the senior RAF officer but nothing happened for what seemed an age until, quite suddenly, he was told that it was all fixed, with a berth booked on a convoy ship taking some of the pilots back across the Atlantic. Then he had to break the news to his parents.

He knew now that he would never forget his mother's face when he told her across the table. It drained of colour, her eyes and mouth open as if watching the ball of smoke and flame that was the Focke-Wulf he had downed that morning. He had broken the news the easy way, the cowardly way, during a family dinner when remonstrance and emotional reactions would be restrained.

'Can I come?' asked his brother, Nicky.

'Why?' asked Ruth, one of his sisters. 'You can fly here.'

'Dropping out of your studies?' said his stepfather. 'That wise?'

'When?' asked his mother eventually.

'I don't know when the ship sails but they want me to report tomorrow week.'

'How long for?' asked Ruth.

'Not sure. Probably till the war ends. It can't go on much longer, they reckon.'

'Will you get seasick?' asked Nicky.

'Probably. I guess the crossing will be the most dangerous bit.'

He had meant it to reassure his mother but it was clear that nothing would do that. Later that evening she came to his room, as he knew she would. She stood in the doorway, quiet and composed.

'Why, Frank?'

He wasn't sure himself. It sounded dangerous and exciting and he wanted to be part of it. It seemed important that the good side won. It was something to do with proving himself, but he didn't want to go into that.

'I guess I feel I can make a contribution. They need pilots and I'm a pilot. It's a good cause, the right cause. We've sent a lot of troops over there.'

'But you could apply to join the Royal Canadian Air Force and go with them.'

That would take longer and he might end up flying hour after monotonous hour searching for U-Boats in the North Atlantic. This way he could be sure of getting into action quickly in one of the new fighters and the RAF had already said they would accept him. 'Same thing,' he said, 'but these are the guys I know and they fixed it. Sooner than I thought, I admit.'

'It would be better to finish your degree, then go if you still want to. You'll be well qualified and maybe more use to them.'

'But the war might be over before I get there.'

'That's what your father said.'

When they had finished their cheddar the colonel suggested they went and sat down, as he put it. He led the way back across the hall into a panelled sitting room, smaller and darker. The blackout curtains were already drawn and the fire laid but unlit. On either side of the fireplace the walls were lined floor to ceiling with books. The light from the table lamp wasn't good enough for Frank to see what they were; they looked old. There was a framed photograph on the mantelpiece of two women sitting on a garden seat like the woman in the painting, but he couldn't see them clearly. The colonel went to sit in one of the worn leather armchairs either side of a matching sofa, but then turned to the desk before the window and selected a pipe from a rack.

'You're not a pipe man?' he asked, as he lowered himself into a chair.

Frank pulled a crumbled pack of Woodbines from his trouser pocket. 'Can't handle them. Maybe I don't have the patience to keep them going. They seem to need a lot of work. Mind you, these things hardly count as cigarettes. More like sawdust. But they're cheap.'

The colonel filled his pipe. 'I took up cigarettes in

the trenches. Up at the front, anyway. In support or reserve I went back to the pipe. More time and space there. You need both for a pipe.'

Sounds of music came from somewhere in the house, modern music, big band stuff. Frank was surprised by an inward lurch of homesickness. They had records like that at home.

'Gramophone,' said the colonel, pointing his pipe stem at the ceiling. 'Wonderful invention. Some people don't like them but they give more pleasure than pain, I think. On the whole.'

'I thought she was going out,' said Frank. Then, feeling that he was referring too familiarly to the colonel's daughter, added, 'Vanessa, the – who was here earlier.'

'No, no, not going out. Not tonight.' The colonel began heaving himself out of his chair. 'Sorry, remiss of me. Port, brandy, whisky?'

Frank hesitated. The wine must have gone to his head and he was on early call in the morning. But he felt all right.

'I'm going to,' continued the colonel. 'Just a nightcap.'

'A whisky and water would go down well, thank you.'

The music stopped. She would be turning the record over now. But where was she doing it and why, dressed like that, on her own? Presumably.

The music started again as the colonel handed Frank his whisky. 'You like this modern stuff?' he asked.

'I'm afraid I do, sir, very much.'

'Not my taste but I don't mind if it's not too loud. Becoming very popular over here. Like everything American. Same in Canada, I suppose?'

'Very much.'

For the next twenty or so minutes the colonel described the main rivers of Kent. There was really no decent trout fishing to be had in the whole county. There were a few in the Medway at Yalding and a few more in their own Beult – two fewer now – but otherwise you had to go farther east to the Stour and Little Stour. The Rother was better but that was some way west, over the Sussex border. The best stretch was between Robertsbridge and Bodiam. Best of all, in that area was the new reservoir at Sedlescombe, the Powdermill Lake, packed with brown trout, but you had to get day tickets and it was too far on a bike, unless he could stay the night.

Frank felt he was falling helplessly and deliciously into a deep pit of tiredness. He would have loved to give in to it, to sink beneath those swelling, welcoming waves, but he had to go. He was feeling the effects of alcohol now, too. It would slow him in the morning, if he had to fly. He stood, feeling a little unsteady.

'I guess I'd better be getting back.' The colonel was

smiling at him. He realised the guy had been saying something and he'd been agreeing without knowing to what. 'Thank you for the fish, sir, for the dinner, for everything. It's real kind of you.'

'Fish whenever you like. Come and eat whenever you like. There's more to talk about, I'm sure.'

They shook hands at the door. The colonel put his other hand on Frank's shoulder. 'Keep your eyes peeled. The Hun in the sun, remember.'

The phrase was so familiar that it took Frank a few seconds to wonder how the colonel knew it. 'Vimy,' he said, turning almost too abruptly as he reached the bottom step. 'Near a place called Vimy. That was where my father was killed. He was a gunner, in the artillery. Have you heard of it?'

He couldn't see the colonel's features because they had turned off the hall light before opening the door, but he sensed they changed. 'Vimy, yes, I knew Vimy. Near there, you say. Not a place called Lens, by any chance?'

'Don't know could've been. I just remember my mother said near Vimy.'

'Lens was a rough one. Very near the end but still a rough one. I thought perhaps – perhaps it might be – we'll talk again.'

Frank groped for his bike in the dark, banging his shin on the pedal. If he'd done it harder, much harder, a damaged shin would have got him off flying tomorrow because he couldn't operate the aircraft pedals properly. But then he remembered he didn't want to be off flying, he wanted to be doing it, with the others.

He pushed the bike along the drive towards the gap in the trees that showed the slightly lighter western sky, not trusting himself to ride in the dark until on the road. When he reached the trees he paused and looked back at the house. The music had stopped but one of the upstairs sash windows was open and, as his eyes adjusted to the dark, he made out the head and shoulders of a woman, leaning out. He couldn't see her features but the shape of her hair was Vanessa's. Her forearms were bare, faintly white. He raised his hand, although doubting she could see him. For a few seconds there was no response, then she slowly raised one hand, palm out, and withdrew.

Chapter Four

They were held in readiness the next morning. Another squadron did a wide sweep early on but found nothing apart from two more flak-ships off the French coast, which they honoured with a wide berth. There was a card game in the Dispersal hut. Frank sat it out, having no interest in cards. Heedless whether he won or lost, he could never feel it had anything to do with him. The Dodger also sat it out, in a corner with Tony, the baby-faced, prematurely balding newcomer, serious and quiet. They were trying to reassemble the gramophone they had dismantled, Tony on his knees and hunched over the detached head that held the needle, silent and intent, while the Dodger swore and expostulated. It was easy to imagine them as boys playing with Meccano; it could not be long since they had.

Frank sat apart, smoking and flicking through a

three-day-old *Daily Mirror*, prized by all ranks for the adventures of Jane, its near-naked cartoon pin-up. He felt tired but had no hangover, confident he could perform as usual but relieved he wasn't asked to. The gramophone reinforced his preoccupation with Vanessa and her solitary music. He couldn't write and thank them for dinner – he had no address, not even the name of the village. He could establish both with a little effort, of course, but he preferred to use it as a reason to call again soon. Ideally with another fish later that day, after they were stood down.

He went outside to stretch his legs in a walk round the hut. It was a day of high broken cloud, significantly cooler than the day before and with an unseasonably chilling breeze. The mechanics lay wrapped in blankets beneath the wings of the waiting Spitfires. The whole aerodrome, not just the smoke-filled Dispersal hut, seemed oppressed by ennui. Nothing was happening, nothing was due to happen, nobody wanted anything to happen but unless it did everything was pointless. Frank lit another cigarette and stood staring at the elms beyond the end of the runway. The only moving thing was the station commander's Hillman, leaving the control tower. Somewhere beyond those trees were the colonel and Vanessa, doing he knew not what, living lives he could not imagine. At least in her case.

Back in the hut the card game had broken up and

there was desultory talk about the war in Italy and
the rights and wrongs of bombing Rome or shelling
Monte Cassino. Patrick, who was as usual sitting
apart and reading a book, called out to Tony.

'Didn't you live in Rome, when your father was
at the embassy?'

The boy looked up, pleased to be addressed, carefully removing the gramophone needle from between
his lips. 'Yes but I was away at school most of the
time. Never got to know it well.'

'That's where I met them, your parents. I remember
it now. Your father helped out when I lost my
passport.'

The telephone rang in the corner booth. Everyone
looked up, ennui instantly dissipated. The orderly's
indistinct responses were the only sounds in the tense
silence. He put the phone down and opened the door
and leant out, without bothering to get up from his
seat. 'Early lunch!' he shouted. 'Show this afternoon.
Report to briefing room 1230 hours.'

Back in the mess they ate their sausages and
mash and drank their tea rapidly, almost in silence.
The lack of detail was ominous, suggesting something big. Only the Dodger kept talking, telling
Tony about a nightclub in London. Frank remembered he had intended to reply to his mother's letter
that morning. He would do it later, definitely, provided he got back. He looked round for Patrick,

hoping he was still his wingman, but couldn't see him.

At 1226 they all heard him. 'All right, swallow and leave. Briefing now.' He was standing in the doorway, holding a folder. They filed into the briefing room with a scraping of chairs and clumping of boots on the wooden floor. The wing commander and one of the intelligence officers were already there, standing before the familiar huge map covering one wall and showing London, the south-east of England, the Low Countries and France as far west as Cherbourg. At least it wasn't a map that stretched into Germany, so it wasn't to be a deep penetration show. Instead, a red ribbon marked a route direct to Amiens and back via Boulogne and Dungeness. Once seated, everyone lit up except the wing commander who took to the platform with his notes and pointing stick. Their smoke formed a cloud around models of German and Allied aircraft suspended from the ceiling. But it did nothing to diminish the glamour of the action photographs on the other three walls of Focke-Wulf 190s and Messerschmitt 109s, with diagrams showing aiming deflections.

'Same as with pheasant or grouse,' Patrick had said when Frank joined the squadron. 'Ever shot driven game?'

'I've shot moose,' said Frank.

Patrick laughed. 'You're the only man here who can say that.' From that day Frank was known as Moose.

The wing commander looked up. Tiredness lined his face but his expression was concentrated and determined. A much-decorated man who spoke quietly and wasted few words, he never needed to call anyone to order. They fell silent.

'This afternoon we are taking part in Circus Number 87, H hour 1355. A raid by over one hundred Flying Fortresses on the Amiens Glissy airfield. The operation has been planned for some time and we are a last-minute addition.' He paused, surveying the young men before him. Like Patrick, he had been through the Battle of Britain and, though probably only a few years older than most of them, he seemed a generation apart. 'We have been honoured,' he added, with the hint of a smile.

Close escort on the approach at 16,000 feet would be provided by fourteen Spitfire squadrons, with another two squadrons providing advance support at 20,000 feet over the target from H hour minus five minutes. Further Spitfire squadrons would provide medium and top cover, the latter at 29,000 feet. The role of their own two squadrons was to provide return cover from Amiens at H hour plus five minutes. Their groans would have been audible had it not been for their respect for the wing commander.

The hurly-burly of a dog-fight was one thing, intense, concentrated and short, but escorting bombers home, often damaged and straggling over many miles of air-space, was more gruelling. German fighters would be thoroughly aroused and probably reinforced. The bombers themselves were another danger, especially the Americans with their poor recognition training and trigger-happy gunners too willing to open up on anything that came near them.

The wing commander enumerated the likely strength of fighter defences in that part of France: getting on for two hundred FW190s and about another hundred ME109s from farther away at Saint-Omer and Fort Rouge. Diversionary attacks by Typhoons and Bostons on Poix airfield and on the docks at Dunkirk would absorb some of the defenders and, it was hoped, distract German radar from the forming up of the Flying Fortresses. It was to be a big show.

The wing commander rearranged his notes, then rapidly read out detailed instructions for timings, call-signs, compass-bearings, heights and homing course. Most pilots scribbled the figures relevant to them on the backs of their hands; a few, including Frank, used notebooks. He usually memorised what he wrote but as a precaution would strap the book to his thigh.

Finally, the wing commander said, 'Right, synchronise watches.' He raised his wrist and waited. 'I have twelve hours fifty-one minutes, fifty-five seconds . . . four . . . three . . . two . . . one . . . twelve hours fifty-two minutes exactly.' He looked up, this time without the hint of a smile. 'Stay alert, gentlemen, eyes peeled. Good luck.'

There was more scraping of chairs and shuffling of boots, then they clambered into the back of the Bedford three-tonner to return to the Dispersal huts. There they emptied their pockets of names, addresses, money, tickets, anything that would indicate location, and put it all in their lockers. Some took out lucky mascots – a lighter, an old coin, a teddy bear – before donning their thick white pullovers, sheepskin waist-coats, thigh-length woollen socks and fleece-lined boots. Frank slipped into his right boot the hunting knife he had brought from home and carried throughout his training and on every mission. He had never crashed, been wounded or shot down and he feared not to take it now. Of course it had no effect – how could it? – but why risk leaving it when everything had been all right so far? Yet he didn't think of himself as superstitious, unlike Tony who had the next locker and always flew with a small, moth-eaten teddy bear. Frank counted that as super-stitious. The knife might actually come in handy if he was shot down and on the run.

He tucked his maps into his boot, then loaded his heavy Smith&Wesson revolver and stuffed the pockets of his life-jacket with emergency rations and his escape kit. Fitters appeared with their parachutes and inflatable dinghies, fixing them in the seats of the aircraft along with helmets, earphones and oxygen masks. Clambering into the cockpit, he felt as he imagined medieval knights must have when mounting their steeds, burdened and ungainly. But perhaps once on their horses they would feel at one with their mounts, nimble, swift and deadly, as he knew he would feel once his wheels left the runway and his Spitfire became an extension of his hands and feet and will.

Tightly wedged, he tested radio, sight and camera-gun, armed cannon and machine-guns, adjusted rear vision mirror and oxygen mask, checked pressure in oxygen bottles, and waited. The squadron call-sign that day was Shield, with Patrick as Shield One. They would start engines at 1322 hours, take off at 1325, orbit until formed up, set course at 1332, fly at zero feet over the Channel, climb on full power to 10,000 feet when crossing the French coast, then rendezvous over Amiens at 25,000 feet. There they would turn 90 degrees to port and steer 047 degrees for five minutes. On the way they would ditch their auxiliary fuel tanks after twenty-five minutes at the signal to 'drop your babies', then take up battle formation.

Still they waited in silence on the runway. Fitters with screwdrivers went from aircraft to aircraft, slowly tightening the detachable panels. Others stood by with their fingers on the auxiliary starter batteries, yet others knelt by the fire extinguishers lying in the grass beside each aircraft. The fire crew sat on the running boards of their fire engine, the medics sat in their ambulance. There were no sounds, no radio chatter. It was as if a spell had been cast upon the entire airfield.

Frank's stomach felt light and empty, despite the recent lunch. He now thought he should have had another pee when they returned to the Dispersal hut. He had thought of it at the time but hadn't wanted one. He didn't really now but worried that knowing he couldn't might persuade him he did. He tried thinking of other things – fishing, the problem with the gears on Roddy's bike, what Vanessa and her father might be doing at that moment. Having lunch, presumably. Would they be sitting formally at that long polished table beneath the painting of the woman in the sun-dappled garden? Or would they eat more humbly and informally at a table in the kitchen he hadn't seen? What would they be talking about; what would they do that afternoon? It was easy to imagine the colonel walking his land, but what would she do? Frank could no more imagine that than he could imagine her dressed differently. She was like a dream figure, existing only as she had briefly appeared, untouchable, unchangeable. Yet they had touched when they met. He recalled the feel of her hand, her warm hand – unless it was simply that his were cold after cycling. It was that hand that she had raised from the window when he left. Unless he had imagined it.

He mentally rehearsed the cockpit drills he had already been through – brakes, trim, flats, contacts, pressure, petrol, undercarriage, radiator. They were all waiting for the signal from Patrick, sitting motionless in his aircraft a few yards away. At 1320 hours his head moved as he glanced at each of the twelve in his squadron. Then his voice came through the still-connected intercom: 'All clear? Switches to On.'

His starter coughed and his propeller began to turn. The fitters sprang to life as if electrocuted, pulling away chocks and batteries, hanging on to wingtips to help the aircraft pivot. Frank was first behind Patrick, who was already taxiing to the runway. The sound of his Rolls Royce Merlin engine, which he loved, filled his head now as it filled the cockpit. There was no room or time for anything else. The other squadron was already lined up at the end of the runway on either side of the wing commander's Spitfire, their propellers sending up clouds of dust. Patrick's squadron fell in behind them in combat formation, Frank now wingtip to wingtip with Patrick. Again they waited, twenty-six in all, engines roaring although only on tick-over, their propellers spinning slowly enough to be visible. The sun broke through the hazy cloud, glinting on the turning blades. In other circumstances it might have been the preliminary to a celebration.

At 1325 a white rocket streaked skywards from the flat roof of the control tower. The wing commander raised his arm and the first squadron moved off as one. Patrick raised his gloved hand and started forward after them, Frank keeping level, his eyes on their almost-touching wingtips. Patrick's tail went up as he opened his throttle. Frank did the same, his aircraft jibbing and bouncing on its narrow undercarriage until the wheels left the ground and everything was smooth. He raised and locked the undercarriage, throttled back, adjusted airscrew pitch, switched to auxiliary tanks. They crossed the road at tree-top height, the roar of their engines almost flattening everything beneath them. A green country bus had stopped and a woman disembarking dropped her shopping bag and clutched at her hat – too late – as wave after wave of aircraft created a thunderous whirlwind, shaking the trees. They skimmed the roof-tops of a village, below the top of the church spire, causing people to duck in the street, hands to their ears, and scattering nearby sheep and cattle. They followed valley bottoms through the low wooded hills of the Sussex Weald, dived up and over the South Downs and quite suddenly were skimming the choppy grey sea, leaving Beachy Head above and behind them.

The wing commander led them even lower, a few feet above the dirty fractious waves. It was uncomfortable and enervating flying, with ceaseless nervous adjustments to maintain height and formation during the buffeting of slipstreams. At 350 knots a moment's loss of concentration would send an aircraft bulleting into the grey waves.

The French coast was a growing smudge through the haze. Their radios, switched to receive only, picked up shouts and calls from the escort squadron already over Amiens. It sounded a hot scrap. At 1350 hours precisely the wing commander's Spitfire rose abruptly and the rest followed as one, climbing steeply on full throttle as the Somme estuary widened beneath them. At 15,000 feet the wing commander broke radio silence with the order to drop babies. Frank pulled his handle and felt his plane jump as if someone had kicked it upwards. Twenty-six near-empty tanks tumbled and spiralled into the woods and fields of France.

Then, as loudly and clearly as if with them in the cockpits, the crisp tones of fighter control in England instructed them to go over to Channel C Charlie. The wing commander acknowledged and they pressed button C on their VHF panels. After some warbling, a familiar controlling voice, the man with the radar, told them to steer zero nine six, adding almost casually, 'Plenty of business over target. Fifty plus bandits fifteen miles ahead, angels three five, over.'

The wing commander acknowledged again and the two squadrons drew apart into wider combat formation. Frank dropped back until he was behind and a little above Patrick. Without turning his head, he could just see the Dodger way off to his right. They were approaching 30,000 feet in a now cloudless sky of pitiless clarity. The ground was shrouded by haze but the limitless blue sky above was stunningly bright. It hurt to breathe and Frank's fingers and toes felt like heavy blocks of ice. In the rarefied air the aircraft rocked slightly, as if on a gentle swell. Along with the cold and the rhythmic, enveloping sound of the engine, it engendered a dream-like unreality. Frank turned up the oxygen to rouse himself.

Control came up again, with the same disturbing and intimate clarity. 'Thirty plus bandits approaching you above. Out.'

Almost simultaneously someone in the other squadron shouted, 'Bandits three o'clock closing fast above!' Patrick shouted, 'Bandits above and behind break right!' Frank recalled afterwards that he had begun to call out, too, having glimpsed the first group as the first pilot shouted, but he never got beyond the word 'bandits' because the roundels of Patrick's Spitfire filled his screen as Patrick banked and climbed. Frank avoided him only by banking sharply left, then heaving on the controls to bank right and follow on full throttle. The centrifugal force pushed him so hard into his seat that for some seconds he could move neither hands nor feet, following Patrick's turning and climbing Spitfire with his eyes only. His goggles pressed painfully on his nose and felt as if they were slipping down his face and skinning it. He couldn't even see the enemy.

He still hadn't seen them when red streaks of tracer flashed between him and Patrick. Patrick abruptly dropped out of sight, leaving Frank climbing almost vertically into the vast and seemingly empty blue. But for the shouts and calls in his headphones, he could have been alone in the universe.

The Hun is always in the sun, it's the one you don't see who gets you; if you don't spot the one who is going to get your mate you're a criminal. The posters on the briefing room wall echoed distractingly in his head. He kicked violently on the rudder bar and heaved with all his strength to get the plane round. As he skidded sideways, more tracer streaked over his dipping right wing and he almost collided with the big black crosses of a Focke-Wulf. He pressed the trigger but his cannon blazed into empty sky.

The next few minutes – perhaps just one, it was impossible to tell – was a fast-moving maze of Spitfires and Focke-Wulfs, criss-crossing lines of tracer, puffs of black smoke, white condensation trails, dirty grey exhaust trails, flashes of cannon and, in the middle, a solitary parachute swaying gently earthwards above a dark, unmoving figure. No one knew where anyone else was or where they themselves were; no one kept the same trajectory for more than a few seconds; no one had a target in his sights for more than one. Way out to Frank's left, level with him, another Focke-Wulf turned towards him. Frank pulled up into a half-roll and briefly, upside-down, had the FW in his sights. He pressed the firing button to give it a prolonged burst, tightening his turn to get enough deflection, his cannon shaking the plane. The FW dived and disappeared, leaving him firing again into emptiness. He dived after him but the German was out of range and faster, anyway.

Frank pulled sharply up and round again, his arm muscles quivering and sweat misting his goggles. He searched the sky for the next enemy but there were none, nor friends either. The scrap had ended as quickly as it had begun; he and the FW must have been the last two in it. He turned again, climbing, and now could see disappearing aircraft in all directions. It was tempting to set a course for home, but for the small matter of the bomber force they were supposed to escort. The scrap had used a lot of fuel but he had enough left not to worry just yet.

There being no point in radio silence now, he called up Patrick. There was no response. It was barely conceivable that Patrick had bought it; he not only led but embodied the squadron with his laconic and paternal style. Brave beyond question, he was more experienced than any of them. But it was more than possible that he would buy it one day. He must know that better than they did. Frank, worried now, was about to call again when Patrick's leisurely tones came reassuringly over the airwaves.

'Delighted you're still with us, Shield Two. Our sheep are scattered and most of the other dogs have gone home. Steer original course and hope we meet up. Over.'

Frank steered 320 degrees, descending to 15,000 feet where the bombers would most likely be. The minute or two of hectic action had dispersed and damaged the escort force before it arrived; radio traffic suggested a much bigger scrap over the target itself and it was likely that the bombers were badly mauled and making their way home piecemeal and unescorted. He felt miserably dissatisfied with his own performance, not because of any particular lapse or error but because he had at no point felt in control of anything. He had been merely reactive, buffeted and knocked about by the actions of others, which he had had no time to anticipate. Perhaps it had been like that for everyone, a messy scrap with neither winners nor losers, but he was not convinced. Pilots like Patrick and the wing commander, perhaps even the Dodger, would come away with at least a rough idea of what had happened, what led to what, why they broke off when they did, what tactics the enemy had adopted. They could somehow be detached while engaged and assemble a picture of the whole. But to Frank it had been as confusing and bruising as the one game of rugby he had been cajoled into during training. Now, with the adrenalin draining from him, he was aware of the cold again, the pains in his feet and fingers, the throbbing in his head and a dangerous sense of detachment from cockpit realities. He was aware, too, of the stealthy and irresistible encroachment of his old enemy, one of his two great secrets, his fear. There was never time for it in action but before and after it could spread from within, a cold, creeping paralysis that tempted him not so much to run away – though he would have loved to do that, to flee somewhere where no one knew him, no one asked anything of him – as to do nothing at all, just to continue as he was, flying on and on until it all stopped.

The only remedy was to make himself focus, make himself do something, anything, one thing at a time, one foot in front of the other, with no thought of how far there was to go. Clouds were coming in from the west and visibility was worsening. He went back up to 17,000 feet and stayed there, looking out for tell-tale smoke trails or dark specks against the white and blue. There was pleasure in manipulating the plane. That was something, enough to focus on and take his mind off the trembling that had returned to his arms. Eventually he saw some dark specks, a couple of miles ahead on a parallel course to his right and at least 2000 feet below. He ascended to 18,000 feet and moved across until directly behind them, increasing speed. Keeping a careful eye on the sky around him, he eased the safety catch off. The planes were moving in and out of broken cloud now, making it harder to count and identify them, but within another minute or so he was confident they were the returning Flying Fortresses. There were six, keeping close for protection though one lagged behind, leaving a haze in its wake. Above and behind them, to the right and left, were two Spitfires. With luck, one of them would be Patrick's, from whom, as wingman, he should not have been separated. Far ahead, when the clouds permitted, was the hazy outline of the French coast. Not far to go now. He throttled back and began a shallow dive well to the right of the right-hand Spitfire, making himself easily visible, obviously unthreatening. He put the safety catch back on and looked about again.

Way out to the left of the gaggle of bombers, at about his own height, he saw a glint of something. At first it was only that, something through the cloud, no more than a distant mountaineer's glasses might glint for half a second in the sun as he turns to view. But it was enough for Frank in one unthinking movement to open his throttle, bring the nose back up and flick off the safety catch. Regaining height, he dipped his left wing to take him in a wide curve above and ahead of where he thought he saw the glint. After a few seconds, briefly between one cloud bank and the next, he saw them as they dived towards the Fortresses and their escorts, aiming to take them from their rear left quarter. There were two, not the usual stubby profiles of FW190s but the more svelte and pointed Messerschmitt 109s, more like Spitfires. As they vanished into the last cloud bank between them and the Fortresses, Frank opened his throttle farther and extended his curve to bring him above and behind where they would emerge, putting him in the same position relative to them as they were to their prey. He still wasn't close enough to identify the Spitfires but called up Patrick's call-sign anyway.

'Hallo Shield One this is Shield Two bandits in cloud seven o'clock break left now over!'

He was still saying it when the ME109s shot out like speeding arrows from the cloud beneath him. The right-hand Spitfire broke up and left, followed by the other. So it was Patrick. The leading ME109 opened fire as Patrick pulled sharply up, leaving the other to slip beneath it and line up directly behind the lagging Fortress. Experienced pilots, obviously. Frank had the leading ME109 in his sights but couldn't get sufficient deflection as it wheeled left and right to follow Patrick's desperate evasions. Patrick flew brilliantly, twisting and turning his aircraft to its limit. The Spitfire was more manoeuvrable and could out-turn the 109 but the German was faster and had the advantage of height and surprise. Twice he fired short bursts into Patrick, the second sending small bits flying off Patrick's rear fuselage. Patrick went into a steep dive, curving right. The 109 closed on him, waiting for the perfect position, confident and oblivious.

Frank had the speed and height he needed. A little more pressure on the rudder brought the 109 into his sights, a fraction more and he had the necessary deflection. He squeezed the firing button at less than 300 yards. There were flashes all along the 109's fuselage and the pilot hurled his plane into a violent turn. Twin fingers of flame leapt upwards, then a great outpouring of black smoke through which spurts of flame showed red and yellow. The plane fell away and Frank was beginning a turn to follow when it exploded in a dazzling flash and ballooning black cloud. As he pulled up to escape the shower of debris the 109's engine spun earthwards in a revolving ball of fire. A wing see-sawed slowly down, like a blown leaf.

Frank looked around as he continued his climb, wary of the other 109. He felt no elation at his kill this time. It had been too clinical, almost too easy.

But he felt pride and pleasure at having saved Patrick, making up for his lapse last time. It was mercifully quick, was his other thought. The pilot would have known his plane was hit and that he was trying to get away, but that was about all. In the next second he was translated into oblivion, eternal oblivion, just like before he was born. There would be nothing left to bury, not a hair, not a fingernail of that mother's son.

Frank looked around. The Fortresses were way off now, strung out towards the coast. They had lost their loose box formation and their straggler; a column of smoke arose from a large tract of woodland behind them. Patrick's Spitfire followed them, keeping right and at a distance, a couple of thousand feet below Frank but flying level and with no sign of smoke. Spasmodic bursts of tracer arced out from the two rearmost planes at nothing Frank could see until he spotted, way over to their left, another plane approaching slowly. It was clearly a Spit, even at this distance, but the Fortresses continued their intermittent bursts, hopelessly out of range.

Frank slowly overhauled Patrick, visibly and obviously, as before. The Fortresses had ceased to fire off by the time he caught up, albeit perhaps only because the approaching Spitfire was partially obscured by cloud. It had presumably chased off the other ME109. As Frank manoeuvred alongside Patrick he could see holes towards the rear of his fuselage but no sign of serious damage. Patrick's pale face turned towards him. He raised one hand and grinned as they crossed the French coast. Frank, relaxing, eased away and up a thousand feet, checking his fuel. There was just about enough to see him home.

The other Spitfire emerged from the cloud base above and ahead of them. Frank saw now that it was Tony. His plane looked unscathed as it lost height and turned, showing its white underbelly like a fish as it went for a position on the far side of the Fortresses. It was still turning when the rear and upper gunners of the nearest Fortress opened up on the exposed belly. Frank saw their tracers ripping into its fuel tank, which immediately billowed black smoke. He shouted into his radio – uselessly because the Fortresses were on another frequency – and heaved his plane towards Tony's. But that was just as useless. Tony was already spiralling and tumbling earthwards in a vortex of smoke and flame. His canopy flew up and away and for an instant his hands and arms reached out of the cockpit as he tried to heave himself up. But the fuselage turned again and he was engulfed by another sheet of red flame. The burning carcasses of him and his plane exploded near the beach south of Calais. The Fortresses were well out over the sea.

Frank wheeled once around the pall of smoke then went after the Fortresses, furious and impotent. But not quite impotent. His thumb was on the firing button as he lined up the last Fortress in his sight. He wouldn't do it, he knew. He didn't intend to do it. But if they gave him an excuse, the slightest excuse, a single round of tracer, he would down them. Then Patrick's Spitfire eased in from the right, between him and the bombers. Patrick wriggled his wings, indicating that Frank should fall in behind. Frank backed off, his heart thumping, sweating again despite the cold. They'd be back in the mess for tea.

Chapter Five

Later, about two and a half hours after Tony had been a living and breathing presence, when they had finished their toast, Patrick got up and nodded to Frank to follow him. Frank was happy to leave the mess. The Dodger was recounting his two near misses and one probable. Everyone else was quiet, but the Dodger hadn't noticed.

It had not been a good mission. True, they had lost only Tony whereas the other squadron had lost two, but the Fortress fleet had been badly mauled, losing a third of its strength. At the debrief the wing commander had been more than usually crisp and critical, describing the bombing as wilfully and shamefully inaccurate. Many Fortresses, meeting heavy flak around the airfield, had veered away or climbed above it and dropped their bombs anywhere. At one point the only planes near the airfield were the covering

Spitfire squadrons, with nothing to cover. Then, because of their avoidance of the target, the bombers had failed to form defensive and defendable formations on the way back. Spreading out over northern France and Belgium, they made easy meat for the Luftwaffe. Our own encounter before reaching the bombers, the wing commander said, was because the diversionary Typhoon attacks had not worked as intended. That is, they had worked but only too well, taking the Germans so completely by surprise that by the time they reacted the diversions were over and the real attack was about to start. Thus, the bombers and escorting fighters had flown into a stirred-up hornets' nest.

Patrick waited for Frank in the mess entrance, by the table where their letters were laid out. It reminded Frank that he still hadn't written to his mother. Patrick picked up a couple of letters.

'Two for Tony. One from home, by the looks of it, the other –' he turned it, studying the postmark – 'unclear. Feminine hand, wouldn't you say?'

Frank looked at the neat, well-rounded script.

'He has – had – a girlfriend,' said Patrick. 'We'll have to send them back with his things. Wondered if you could give me a hand with that.'

They walked through the huts to Tony's, which he shared with five others. The cloud had thickened and there was a fretful, inconstant breeze. The windsock alternately stiffened and sagged and the usual airfield activities – planes and all manner of things were endlessly moved, anchored, hidden, worked on, moved again – seemed piecemeal and subdued.

'Not something we normally do, I know,' continued Patrick. 'Clerks in the station commander's office see to it. Miserable job. But I know his people, you see. Wouldn't want anything to go to them they wouldn't want, nothing upsetting. Bad enough losing him but then to find – well, you never know what, something in his stuff they'd rather not have known about – makes it even worse. Affects the way they remember him.' He held up a folded canvas bag. 'Got this from the station office. I have to make a list and you have to witness it, if you wouldn't mind. Best get it over with while the others are still in the mess.'

The hut, with its narrow iron bedsteads, plain table, standard lockers, hangers for uniforms and cylindrical coke stove, was identical to Frank's: clean, efficient, cheerless. Tony's bed was at the far end. Gingerly at first, they emptied his bedside drawer, then his locker, then the pockets of his clothes. Next they took his pyjamas from the bed and stripped it. Everything belonging to the RAF they stacked at one end of the bed, everything personal at the other. His uniforms and kit would be returned to stores, his possessions sent to his next of kin. They worked slowly, with none of the impersonal briskness of the clerks, who were used to it. It felt unpardonably intrusive, almost illicit. They separated the personal into two piles, the smaller comprising things they decided not to return, or were unsure about: non-issue underclothes, an opened packet of contraceptives with one remaining, a magazine of women modelling underwear, a dozen or so opened letters in the same feminine hand as the one they had, an RAF notebook in which were pencilled a number of incomplete poems, or perhaps versions of the same poem.

Patrick leafed through it. 'Didn't know he wrote poetry. Did you?'

'No. I didn't know him well.'

'His father does, or did. Published, I think. Question is, would he have wanted his parents to see them?'

'Depends what they're like, I guess.'

Patrick shook his head over the pages, without looking up. 'Pretty much the sort of thing most of us would do if we allowed ourselves to lapse into verse. Sincerely felt, no doubt, but sincerity is never enough, is it? Sadly.' He held out the book. 'Want a look?'

'I never read poetry.'

'Don't like it?'

'Can't read slowly enough.'

Patrick closed the book with a smile and put it on the NOK pile, along with photos, pen, cash, address book, wallet, cheque book, ties, shirts and socks. 'I think they should see it. They'd probably want to. They may not know he wrote and for them sincerity is probably more than enough, poor folk. But these are more of a problem.' He held up the love-letters. 'Awful thing is, I half want to read them. If I didn't at all I'd be happy to flick through them and check there's nothing too upsetting for his parents. But because I have a prurient interest in seeing what it's like for other people, I'm reluctant. Such an intrusion.' He smiled.

Frank, who had never sent or received a love-letter, was equally reluctant and probably more curious. It touched on his other secret, his virginity. 'Shouldn't we just send them back to his girlfriend, along with today's?'

'Still have to look inside to get the address. But if that's all we do, I suppose it's all right.' He put them down without opening any and picked up Tony's brown wallet, taking out the picture of a smiling blonde girl wearing a roll-necked jersey. 'Lucky Tony. Or was.' He put it back and counted out some pound notes. 'Three quid here, plus the loose change in that jacket pocket. That makes three pounds seven and nine. Note and witness it.' He replaced everything and sat staring at the pile. 'Hope whoever goes through my stuff when my number's up will be as considerate as us.'

Frank was surprised and dismayed. 'You reckon it's coming, then?'

Patrick smiled again, almost indulgently. 'Would've today, but for you.'

He didn't like to think of Patrick as vulnerable. He could accept his own vulnerability – was only too well aware of it – so long as there was someone who wasn't, someone dependable who would keep him up to the mark. He picked up Tony's uniform dress shoes. 'But that's the same for all of us, every time. There's always someone who gets someone else out of trouble.'

'I'll give the love-letters to the clerks. They'll know what to do. Must be a drill for it. Drill for everything in the RAF.'

Afterwards Frank went to his hut and wrote to his mother. He had intended to go fishing but there wasn't time now. He would have caught a fat trout and taken it to the colonel, or, at least, to the colonel's house. Vanessa would have received it with surprise and admiration, they would have eaten together, themselves alone, and then – but then he imagined the distancing brightness of her switch-on hostess's smile, how desirable yet unapproachable she was in her stockings and smart clothes, the enigma of her appearance in the darkened window. He tried to imagine being in bed with her but he couldn't, not with any particularity, partly because he couldn't imagine what that was like with anyone and partly because, in his mind, she was forever withdrawing, closing the door, fading like the light outside the hut window.

Those stockings, hard to find in England now, must surely have been given her by someone. Most likely an American serviceman. It was impossible to imagine she had no admirers and he hated to think of her with them. He couldn't be the only virgin in the RAF but it felt like it, from the way the others spoke. This secret, like his fear, he nursed closely. It was even more shameful – fear was at least understandable and, he was sure, privately shared by many. But being a virgin made him feel he was living under false pretences, pretending to be a man without having fully qualified. He feared being killed without having done it, as if even in death he would be incomplete. Tony had done it, clearly. That must have made it easier to die.

It ought to have been easier to get rid of his virginity than his fear. He had tried a couple of times in Canada and once nearly succeeded – perhaps he would have if he'd stayed. Since arriving in England he had had only one chance to try again, during a couple of days' leave in London between finishing training in north Wales and joining the squadron in Kent. He had taken a room in a hotel near Paddington station that smelt of damp carpet, stale cigarette smoke and old dust. Someone on the course had said there were plenty of prostitutes around

Paddington and that the more exotic and desirable-sounding high-class call girls were available there. During two days of lonely and frustrated discontent, feeling more homesick than at any time since docking in Liverpool, he had failed to find any high-class call girls. Indeed, he had no idea how to go about it, assuming that the names and telephone numbers found in call-boxes were not what his informant had in mind.

He roamed the streets without result, identifying women he thought might be prostitutes but then avoiding them. The drabness of the city, the bomb sites with their peeling walls of half-demolished buildings, like private indecencies made public, and the hunched, pale penury of many of the women, diminished his desire and made him question why he was doing it at all. But he carried on, stubbornly. Late during the second evening after an air-raid that had had happened mainly somewhere else, a girl's voice had called out from an alleyway by a pub that was closing. 'Got a light, love?'

He saw a pale face in the dark and felt in his pocket for his matches. 'Guess I have.'

'Are you American?'

'Canadian.'

'I like Canadians.'

As he went to strike she cupped his hands in hers and pulled him into the alleyway. 'Mind the blackout.

Coppers come round here at closing time.' The flare showed a thin face with a prominent nose and a fringe of dark hair. Her cigarette was mostly smoked already, little more than a fag-end. She turned her head as she exhaled. 'You got anywhere we can go?'

'I'm in a hotel near here.'

'Which one?'

He told her, aware now that he was merely experimenting with himself. Once the prospect ceased to be abstract, an imagined scene with an imaginary woman, all desire left him.

'Cost you more,' she said. "Long as you can get me in. Otherwise it's here. Don't have a place of me own.'

The hotel desk was not manned and, from what he had observed, a challenge was unlikely anyway. Most of the other guests seemed to use it as a place of assignation. She stood looking round as he closed and locked the bedroom door. 'Don't give you room to swing a cat here, do they? What'd it cost?'

He told her.

'Blimey.'

She wore a blue high-shouldered jacket that was too big for her and a tight green skirt. Her shoes, which had probably been cream, were worn and scuffed, her thin legs bare. There was a new smell in the room, which he assumed was her.

She looked at him. 'Pay in advance, I'm afraid. No

69

reflection, I do it with everybody. I have to. Some men think they can help themselves to what they want and do a runner.'

She took off her clothes as if for an RAF medical. Her underclothes were a washed-out grey and she was as skinny as a stick. She was the first naked woman he had seen, apart from photographs surreptitiously passed around at school, and he stared with more curiosity than desire. She lay on the narrow bed. 'Come on, then, let's get on with it.' She smiled with what was probably intended as teasing encouragement. Some teeth were missing, others discoloured. 'Not shy, are you?'

He undressed and squeezed onto the bed beside her. She rested her head on his shoulder and began fondling him. He could smell her hair when it fell across his face. He carefully removed it from his mouth and nose. He had never felt less aroused.

'Bit knackered tonight, are we, love? Been having a bit too much of it?'

'Let's talk for a while.'

She let go and sat up. 'Talking's all right, I don't mind that. Still cost you, though, 'cos it's still my time. Got any fags?'

He took his cigarettes from his battledress trouser pocket, found a tin ashtray on the window ledge and sat on the bed with her.

'Senior Service, I ain't had one of these for ages,'

70

she said. 'Don't 'alf cost, don't they? I thought you'd have some American or Canadian ones.'

'Can't get them over here. Not in the NAAFI anyway.'

'I had a packet of twenty once, off of an American. Peter something, they was called. Whole packet, I had.'

'Peter Stuyvesant?'

'Yeah, something like that. My old man works in the NAAFI. He gets fags what fall off the backs of lorries, like.'

'Your father works in the NAAFI?'

'No, me husband. In Malta, he is. Good riddance. Hope he stays there.'

'Does he – does he know what you—'

'What I get up to? No need, is there? I don't know what he gets up to. Don't want to, neither. Anyway, a girl's got to put a penny in her purse, hasn't she? Starve to death if I lived off what he sends me. Right old Scrooge, he is.'

They talked through two cigarettes each. She lived in Bayswater, which she said was not far away and meant she could walk to work. They had no children and lived in her mother-in-law's rented house. She had always lived in Bayswater and had never been to any other part of London except to Notting Hill sometimes, for the market. She would like to go to America or Canada 'with all them big swanky cars and polar bears'. Her mother-in-law was nearly deaf and blind and was anyway away with the fairies most of the time and had no idea whether she was there or not. It was a relief to get out of the house.

She stubbed out her second cigarette. 'Time I got back to work if there's nothing going on here, then.' She flicked his penis and grinned. 'Wouldn't mind a few more like you. Easy money.'

She dressed swiftly while he counted out the money. 'Ta, love. Get a good night's sleep. You'll be all right in the morning.'

He began to dress. 'I'll show you down. It's a bit—'

''S all right, know it like the back of me 'and round here. Sleep well.'

The door closed, leaving him relieved but restless and discontented. He half dressed and then, hearing no one about, crept along the corridor to the toilet, where he masturbated, proving to himself that it was indeed still all right. When he returned to his room and reached for another cigarette he found she had taken the packet.

Later that evening Frank left the letter to his mother in the post room by the station office, then sauntered over to the mess. The moment he entered, he wished he hadn't. It was crowded and noisy, awash with beer and thick with smoke, the bar almost hidden behind the crush of blue serge uniforms. The Dodger was at the piano in the corner, with a group around him banging their glasses to the bawdy version of *Lili Marlene* he was thumping out. He seemed a gifted pianist – Frank was no judge but had heard him in more reflective mood playing long passages of classical music from memory – who preferred clowning. *Lili Marlene* ended with a great shout by virtually everyone in the bar. Frank was about to withdraw when the Dodger spotted him.

'Moose – Moosey, old lad!' he shouted, holding up his arm. 'Owe you a pint for that Hun. Come and have a pint.' He stood abruptly, brimming with beer and good fellowship. His chair fell over behind him. 'Lemme get you your pint. Always pay my debts. You the same for me next time.'

He came over and put his arm round Frank, then barged a way for both of them through the massed shoulders and backs to the bar. There was more singing, in which Frank pretended to join, then an argument as to whether brunettes or blondes were more likely to be goers. The Dodger made the case for redheads and was interrupted by someone who shouted that he said it only because he was ginger. The Dodger protested that gingers were always being got at, someone emptied someone else's beer on his head to help his hair change colour, then there was a call for British Bulldog. Frank, jostled and quiet in the clamour, tried to look engaged while thinking of

Tony's blonde girlfriend and wondering who would break the news to her. The RAF would inform only NOK of a death and if Tony's parents didn't tell her – assuming they knew about her – she would simply never hear, unless the RAF returned her letters to her, with a note. As the teams formed up for British Bulldog he saw again Tony's briefly flailing arms as he struggled to get out of his cockpit before the flames engulfed him.

He slipped out of the mess into the welcome dark and fitful gusts of rain. It was more wind than rain but occasional drops peppered his head and face refreshingly. He wanted to stretch his legs and so walked past the huts and across the wet grass towards the airfield perimeter. A lane ran parallel the other side of the fence, partly screened by a belt of young conifers. It was normally quiet, with just the odd cyclist, tractor or horse, but as he approached he heard the subdued growl of multiple engines on low revs. When he was close enough to see through the trees he made out the high black bulks and shaded blackout lights of Army lorries rumbling along nose to tail. Another division heading for camps near the coast, presumably, one of many recent and seemingly endless convoys, sometimes taking days and nights to pass. The Day, the invasion of Europe, the opening of the second front, must be close.

The   lorries   were   canvas-backed   Bedford

three-tonners, probably an infantry division. Through a gap in the trees he made out the faces of young soldiers, crammed onto benches in the backs, festooned with rifles and kit, lolling at unlikely angles, dozing or comatose, their heads resting on each other and rocking to the movements of the lorries. None spoke and the eyes of those who were awake stared dully at the vehicle behind. It was a vision of a catacomb of corpses, thrown in anyhow.

He left the convoy to its destiny. Across the airfield in the dispersal areas, Spitfires rested on their tail wheels, long noses pointing towards the scurrying, moonlit clouds. There was virtually no chance of anyone flying now but still their ground crews lay huddled beneath them, wrapped in groundsheets. He walked past unnoticed, following the perimeter to where the ground dropped away, revealing, in daylight, a full view of the Romney Marsh. It was a solid dark mass now. Above it the clouds alternately obscured and displayed ever-changing spaces of lighter, fading sky. Frank stood, the intermittent fine sprays of rain wafting like blessings against his face.

Eventually he turned to continue his walk but after a few yards he stopped, assailed by the smell of cigar smoke. 'Rather you walked round me than over me,' said Patrick. 'Don't much fancy being trampled by a moose.' The dark clump ahead moved as Patrick stood, his cigar cupped in his hand. 'Often sit here last thing, clear the mind, pollute the lungs. Wet bum tonight.'

'I almost walked into you.'

'Unforgivable to light up, of course, especially for the squadron leader. But I'm careful and no one's ever caught me at it before.' He cupped both hands to his mouth and the stub glowed within them. 'I guess there are worse sins,' he added after exhaling, 'not available to us.'

'They were to Tony.'

'Yes, if fornication's a sin. Not sure the RAF would have a view on that, unless it were fornication between ranks. Anyway, good luck to them, poor sinners both. Take it while you can. He won't be doing much more of it, that's for sure. Unless there's fornicating in heaven.'

'I was close to downing that Yank.'

'I know, I saw you were, saw you lining up. That's why I intervened. Understandable, felt the same myself, but it won't do, not while there's still Germans to shoot down.'

'What will happen about it?'

'Nothing. That is, we'll put in an official complaint, they'll deny it, bums on office seats will shuffle paper between them and we'll all forget about it. Except his people and his girlfriend, of course. But they won't be told; they'll assume he was shot down by the Luftwaffe. Better that way. Even worse if they knew.' He bent and pushed his cigar stub into the grass, grinding it with his boot. They walked on, side by side.

'Had enough of the mess tonight?' said Patrick.

'I just – well, yeah, I guess so.'

'Too much for everyone, sometime or other. We all need some escape.'

'Except the Dodger. Seems to suit him.'

'Horses for courses. Some escape by immersion, diving deeper, never thinking about it. Others like you and me have to come up for air now and again, sit on the bank, take a few breaths.'

'I didn't realise you did.'

'That's the thing about being in it, you don't notice those who climb out. Talking of banks, sitting on, how's your fishing going? Any luck?'

Frank soon found himself talking about the colonel and Vanessa. It was an unexpected relief.

'Enigmatic,' said Patrick.

'She is, yes. I don't get what's going on. Something is, but I just don't get it.'

'I meant him, your colonel. Sounds as if he knows more than he's letting on, keeping something back.'

'Maybe, maybe.' Frank hadn't thought much about the colonel. 'Maybe they're both spies, trying to get information out of me.'

Patrick laughed. 'Pretty disappointing Mata Hari, leaving you alone with her father.'

Frank was in bed before the British Bulldog players returned. They were noisy enough but too bruised and tired to be rowdy and there were no pranks or high jinks. The hut fairly swiftly settled down and soon the only sounds that came to his ears, as he lay awake wondering again whether he would die a virgin, were those of sleeping men and the distant rumble of the three-tonners.

Chapter Six

It was a week before he called again on the colonel, a week of low cloud, rain, poor visibility and inconclusive but dangerous daily missions. They did sweeps over northern France, giving the airfields a wide berth but concentrating on railway goods yards and military sites. In order to see, they were forced beneath the clouds, which meant they could report that German anti-aircraft defences were increasingly concentrated and effective. They lost another pilot – Alun, from Wales – and had several planes seriously damaged. The Luftwaffe made few appearances but Patrick and Frank shot up a long goods train of camouflaged tanks and guns outside Abbeville. Its three anti-aircraft platforms were taken by surprise because their approach was so low and fast, shielded by a road bridge which they almost clipped. The arthritic old engine, belching great gouts of smoke out of all proportion to its size, exploded gratifyingly.

'Pity the crew were French,' said Patrick afterwards. 'If only they'd seen us coming they might have had time to jump off.'

During the following two nights Frank awoke sweating and shaking after dreaming of the red brick parapet of the road bridge leaping at him and filling his screen.

On the Sunday, after they had been stood down for the day, Frank had time to fish again. It was another day of low cloud and drizzle which never quite qualified as rain nor ever quite stopped but was silently, insistently dampening, as if the very air were breeding rain. The airfield windsock hung wet and limp.

'Like a flaccid cock after a party,' said the Dodger.

Roddy's bike was still round the back of the hut where Frank had left it. The saddle was warped enough to hold water. He rubbed it down, tied his rod to the crossbar, slung his kitbag over his shoulder and set off along the airfield slip-road. Once through the barriers he had at first to follow the lane used by the convoy. It was clear now and he pedalled in a silence broken only by the regular tick of the Sturmey Archer in top gear until two Army one-tonners, Humber signals trucks bristling with aerials, drenched him by passing within inches of his handlebars as he rode through a large puddle. He heard someone laugh.

He returned to the spot where the colonel had found him. The long grass soaked his trousers but he didn't mind once he was standing beneath the willows, hanging lower now because of the rain. The green solitude soaked into him, the river was opaque and the only sounds were dripping leaves and the hiss of rain on water. The cattle were nowhere to be seen. He cast and re-cast, giving himself over to the gentle mesmerism of the river with its ever-widening and ever-fading raindrop rings.

The trout surprised him when it took his fly. There was a lively struggle after that first and always thrilling tug on the line, but not a long one and he soon had it flapping on the grass at his feet. He despatched it with his priest, then knelt in the wet grass and held it with both hands. It was no larger than the others but big enough for his purpose. He wrapped it in dock leaves and laid it carefully in the bottom of his kitbag, then washed his hands of its clear slime. It would have been better to have two but he didn't want to delay.

This time he cycled up the drive, leaning his bike against the shed as before. The black car in the shed was, he now saw, a Bentley. Also as before, there was no swift response to his pull on the stiff iron bell-pull. He pulled again, provoking a muffled bark from within, and waited hopefully for the sounds of high heels on the parquet floor. There were no sounds but after a few seconds the door opened abruptly.

Vanessa's smile switched on immediately. 'Frank, what a nice surprise.' She looked at the dead fish he was holding, wrapped in dock leaves. 'What have you got there? Just the one today?'

''Fraid so. Just thought I'd leave it with you.' He noticed she had flat-soled shoes this time, with tweed skirt, blouse and cardigan.

'That'll never do. You must taste your own catch. The colonel will be delighted. Come in.' She stood back, looking him up and down. 'Lord, how wet you are. Did you have to jump into the river after it?'

'I guess it's wetter than it looks out there.'

'Always wetter on a bike, anyway, isn't it? Let me have your cap and jacket. I'll put them by the stove. Give me the fish first.'

'My shoes are soaking. Shall I—?'

'They're all right, just wipe them. Come through to the kitchen.'

She took the trout and led him across the hall and through a door behind the stairs. The kitchen was large and high. Everything in it looked old and well-worn but it was tidy. There was a large black range at one end and a scrubbed deal table with odd chairs in the middle. A floor-to-ceiling dresser, full of crockery, occupied half of one wall. Tinker, the blind spaniel, got up slowly from the rug before the range and resumed his devoted sniffing of Frank's trousers. She carried the trout into the scullery at one side, saying over her shoulder, 'Put your things on the rack above the oven. Not on it – it's too hot.'

She still made him feel a generation younger. He lowered the rack and draped his battledress jacket on it, hanging his cap on the end. At least he knew his blue RAF-issue shirt was clean.

She slit and sluiced the trout with brisk efficiency in the shallow stone sink. 'Your trousers look pretty well soaked too but I suppose you'd better keep them on.' This time her smile showed her crooked and overlapping eye-teeth. But at least they were clean and there were plenty of them, unlike the girl in Paddington.

He smiled back. 'I guess so.'

'You see that bell on the window ledge? If you open the door and step outside and ring it a couple of times he'll probably hear it. He's a bit deaf, so give it a vigorous shake.'

It was an old hand-bell, the sort used by teachers in the junior school playground back home. He stepped out onto the long wide lawn, bordered at the end by shrubbery and six tall elms and at the sides by high brick walls. At the bottom there were a couple of sheds and a greenhouse with rain running off it. He stood on the brick path and rang the bell vigorously. Rooks started up from the elms, cawing, and a small bird darted from the bush near his feet. The ringing faded, leaving only the rain.

'I should come back in if I were you,' she called. 'He's probably in the potting shed. He'll come in a minute. Unless you like standing in the rain.'

He came back into the kitchen. 'I didn't mean to impose myself on you for dinner.' It was unconvincing even to his own ears.

She paused at the sink, holding the gutted fish. 'Of course you must stay. The colonel will be delighted. We see little enough company now as it is.' She raised her eyebrows. 'Unless we're too boring for you?'

It was the reassurance he sought but he couldn't resist continuing. 'No, no, really, it's just that – well, one trout isn't much to go round and I don't want to eat into your rations. Especially as I can eat all I like back at base.'

'So long as you don't mind trout with rabbit. We get lots of rabbits and masses of stuff from the garden. There's a large vegetable garden beyond the wall. Too much, in fact, especially since Matthew, our gardener, was called up. Have to do it all ourselves now. Though quite what Matthew contributes to the defence of the realm it's hard to imagine. He was the slowest worker I've ever seen and much too nice to kill anyone.' She laughed as she washed her hands. 'Why

84

don't you go down and fetch him? He should have heard but he doesn't always and he often dithers. Take that coat.'

She nodded at an old brown raincoat hanging from the kitchen door. He noticed her teeth again and wondered whether he would ever be able not to notice them. In Canada people's teeth were whiter and straighter.

He draped the coat over his shoulders. 'My father's a bit deaf, too. My stepfather, that is.'

She smiled again as she came towards him, drying her hands. 'Oh, he's not my father. And he's not that deaf, either. Not very. It's more that if he's concentrating on something he doesn't seem to notice anything else.'

'I thought it was strange that you called your father the colonel. A bit formal. Thought it must be an English custom.' He paused to give her the chance to say what their relation was but she hung up the towel and took three plates from the wooden rack over the sink.

'Tell him I'm pouring drinks before dinner. That'll bring him running.'

The greenhouse was long and very full, built as a lean-to against the wall. Beyond it was a black wooden shed with a single window and an open door through which Frank could smell the colonel's pipe smoke, sweet and heavy in the saturated air. The colonel was seated on a high stool at a bench, wearing thick brown corduroys and a shapeless old tweed jacket, his blunt fingers pressing the earth around a plant in a large pot. His pipe – a straight one this time – was held between his teeth. His face looked redder and more wrinkled than Frank remembered, his blue eyes more rheumy. He looked up at Frank without surprise.

'Ah. Welcome back. All in one piece?'

'Guess so, sir.' Frank tried briefly and not very hard to imagine the colonel and Vanessa making love. He didn't like to picture it. But if she wasn't his daughter, what else could she be? A niece? An orphaned god-daughter? Some sort of paid help?

The colonel pushed more soil into the pot. 'Any luck today?'

'One, not very big. I didn't intend to invite myself to dinner but Vanessa—'

'Of course you must, of course. You don't need to bring anything, anyway.'

'It'll go with the rabbit, she says.'

'No shortage of rabbits around here.' He took his time, breathing loudly through his nose as he pressed compost in with a small trowel. The rain drummed on the shed roof. 'Been busy?'

'Here and there, nothing major. Poor flying weather. Vanessa's just pouring drinks before dinner.'

'Suppose you have to go low, don't you, under this cloud? Forces you into the flak. Very unpleasant.'

'Livens things up a bit, that's for sure.'

The colonel eased himself off the stool, wiping his hands on his corduroys. 'Couldn't lift it down for me, could you? Put it with the others outside the door. Damned heavy when they're full, these big ones, and my shoulder's been playing up.'

It was heavier than Frank anticipated but he managed to place it alongside four or five others without humiliation. 'What is it?'

'Box. Pretty hardy but needs a good start.'

An idea came to Frank. 'Vanessa says you've lost your gardener?'

'Matthew? Yes. Agreeable young chap. Old village family. Steady enough worker as long as you're around to keep an eye on him. Sort of chap whose Army report would read, "Works well under supervision." Don't know how he'll do in the regiment.' He took his pipe from his mouth. 'I served with his father, who was gassed at Ypres. Survived the war but his lungs were no good and he died about ten years ago.'

They dined in the kitchen on casseroled rabbit and vegetables, preceded by the neatly-divided trout as an hors d'oeuvre. They had a bottle of claret with the rabbit. 'Unpardonable extravagance in wartime,' said the colonel as he poured. 'Vanessa disapproves, of course, but she can't argue when there's a guest, can you, my dear?' His blue eyes twinkled faintly. 'Got the habit in France during the last show. Unable to drop it, no matter how hard I try. May as well drink what's left of the cellar before a bomb lands on it. Another lesson from the last show.'

Vanessa smiled at the colonel and raised her eyebrows at Frank.

'Are you still in touch with anyone from your old regiment?' asked Frank.

'One or two. Only fifteen of the originals who volunteered in 1914 came back. Out of eight hundred. Some have died since then, of course, like Matthew's father. I was already in the Territorials and got drafted into the eighth battalion early on so I count as an original.'

'I guess you had it worse than we do, all that hand-to-hand fighting.'

The colonel chewed slowly. 'Not necessarily. Your war ain't over yet, remember. When it is, go back through your squadron records and see what your casualty rate was. You may be unpleasantly surprised.'

'So long as I'm around to do it.'

'I'm sure you will be.' Vanessa took his empty plate and put it noisily on hers. The colonel hurried to finish his. When Frank made to get up to help she waved him down. 'Don't, this is my job. No cheese today, I'm afraid, but there is tea or coffee. What passes for coffee, anyway.'

She ran water into the sink and put the plates in

to soak. Then she put the kettle on the stove and set out three coffees. 'If you'll both excuse me, I'll take mine upstairs.'

Her briskness felt like disapproval but Frank couldn't think what he'd done to merit it. It was almost a disease, this English habit of not saying what you thought. It was impossible to know how to respond. As she left the room he rose from the table but she swept out without noticing. The colonel seemed unperturbed, his spaniel features blandly unknowing, or perhaps unacknowledging. He took his pipe and tobacco pouch from the dresser and fished unhurriedly in his corduroys pocket for a battered lighter that looked as if it was made of brass.

'Your father – did he join the Canadian Expeditionary Force or the British Army?'

'I don't know, sir. I could write to my mother and find out. He was in the artillery, I know that.'

'Not the infantry? You're sure of that?'

'Pretty sure, I could write my mother and find out.'

'Do you know when he was killed at Lens – you did say Lens, didn't you?'

'Vimy. Near Vimy.'

'Could it have been September 1918?'

'Could have been I don't know. I was born after the war and I know he was killed not long after he got to France, right near the end of the war.'

'When did your mother re-marry?'

'That must have been – let me see – around 1922, I guess. She met my stepfather at a market. Always says she was bidding for some steers and he came with them.' He was happy enough to talk about his background but it was unusual to be asked. Most people in England showed little detailed curiosity once he'd told them he came from Canada and they'd told him all they knew about his country and named everyone they knew who had gone there, as if he was sure to have met them. But his mind was more on Vanessa. She must have put on one of her records again because dance music – an unfamiliar number – reached them faintly in the kitchen.

The colonel tamped down his pipe, his thick fingers apparently impervious to hot ash. 'I may have known your father.'

The music ceased and the long case clock in the hall struck. It was raining harder now, beating against the kitchen windows. Perhaps she was turning the record over. Frank paused in the act of taking out a cigarette. 'You did? How?'

'The Frank Foucham I knew came from a farming family the other side of Tonbridge. Yeoman farmers, but big for this part of the world. Owned a number of butcher shops. He was secretly engaged to a local girl, Maud. His father found out, the family didn't approve and his father bought some land in Canada and sent him out there to turn it into a farm. Then

90

the war came and Maud, despairing of hearing from Frank and thinking he'd given her up, married someone else.' He paused. 'She married me. She wrote and told him and some time afterwards he joined up and was killed. Hard to believe its not the same chap. Such an unusual name. Though I must say I didn't know he'd married. That's Maud in the drawing room, that's her portrait. Use this.'

He pushed his lighter across the table. It was a primitive contraption, with a worn brass body and a top that slid on and off. Frank lit up. 'That's a mighty steep coincidence, sir. If it's the same Frank Foucham. My mother calls him Frank though I think his real name was Francis, Francis W. Foucham. I was baptized in memory of him.'

'Ask your mother. A Steep coincidence, as you say, that there could have been two Frank Fouchams killed in the same sector of the front right near the end of the war.'

'Should be possible to check that. Regimental records.'

'And he was definitely in the infantry, your father?'

Frank assumed the colonel could not have been listening.

'No, sir, not the infantry, the artillery. He was a gunner.'

'But two Fouchams? There can't have been two who went out to Canada and came back and got killed at more or less the same place at the same time.'

'But my father wasn't out from England, his mother was. His father was French Canadian, like I said.' He pushed the lighter across to the colonel. 'He didn't come out from England.'

The colonel seemed not to register this. 'Frank's parents would be dead but he had two brothers. There's a butcher of that name in Tonbridge and another in Tunbridge Wells but I don't know whether the family still owns them. That was his lighter.'

Frank took the lighter back, rubbing his thumb over its worn surface. It was simple and rugged, qualities he admired. 'You knew him well, your Frank? You were buddies?'

The colonel nodded. 'He made that; made it himself.'

'He must've got the flint and wheel and wick from somewhere.'

'From another lighter, of course. He made the case. Fashioned it from a shell case.'

Of course, thicker metal, which would account for the weight. Frank continued to fondle it. He preferred new things to old things though occassionally he came across a tool or implement, or an old chair, or a knife, that was so eloquent of human contact that you felt it was trying to speak to you. 'He gave it to you then, this Frank Foucham?

The colonel hesitated. 'It was with him when he was killed. On his body. It should have gone to his next of kin, your mother, but – we were friends, you see. I wanted a memento. Keep it, it's yours now.'

Frank let the reference to his mother go. The old man seemed unable to comprehend contradiction. 'Well, that's – that's kind of you, sir, but I can't, not after all this time. He was – he was your friend, nothing to do with me.'

'You have it. I've got other lighters. You must have it.'

'But I—'

'Keep it. Your mother will be pleased. Take that as an order from a senior officer.'

'She would, I'm sure, but I have to tell you I reckon it couldn't have been my father, not really.' But as he looked into the colonel's bloodshot eyes, earnest and imploring, he felt he couldn't – shouldn't – insist. There was something beyond or behind the old man's error, something fragile and necessary. Anyway, there was no harm in letting him live with his illusion, if that's what kept him happy.

'Thank you, sir, I'm grateful, very grateful.' He cupped the lighter in his hands, polishing its sides with his palms. He had never been very curious about his real father, whose existence seemed more an intellectual concept, like evolution or the speed of light, than anything personal to him. It would be different now, he thought. He would take an interest, find out things. This old bit of metal, worn with age and use, was it's unknown maker made real. He would find something similar of his father's. For a few minutes it took his mind off Vanessa.

The colonel didn't appear to want to dwell on the last war and so they talked for a while about the present one, until Frank sensed that the old man was tiring. 'Guess I'd better be getting back.'

They stood in the hall while he put on his almost dry jacket. The music had stopped but there was no sign of Vanessa. 'Please thank Vanessa for me.'

'Thank her yourself,' she said, coming down the stairs. 'But there's no need. Thank you for coming and adding variety to our diet.' She held out her hand. 'At least the rain has left off a bit. You shouldn't get too wet. Come again soon and bring one or two with you, if you like. We have a gramophone, as you may have gathered, and I know how much you boys like a bit of music.'

'Thanks, I'll do that.' He loved the way she pronounced 'gramophone' and 'gathered', almost prissy in their precision yet so sexy. Her hand felt cold and small, but her grip was quite firm. He let go, worried about holding it too long. 'They – we – do like a bit of music, yes. We don't hear much. Make a change from the mess piano.'

'Come any time,' said the colonel. 'No need to bring a fish. We don't demand entry tickets.'

'But if there's more than one of you and they would like to be fed and if you get the chance, do telephone,' she said. 'Two-o-two, same exchange as you.'

'Thanks, I'll do that.' He bent to tuck his trouser bottoms into his socks, wondering how she knew.

'You need cycle clips,' said the colonel. 'Must have some somewhere.'

'Long socks do the trick.' He straightened, hesitating over whether to say it. He looked at Vanessa. 'The garden – you said you had no help now – maybe I could come and help out. I don't know much about plants but I can use a pick and shovel.'

'That's very kind—'

'You mustn't—'

The colonel and Vanessa both spoke at once, and both stopped and laughed. She looked at Frank, still smiling. 'Do,' she said.

Chapter Seven

On the raid the next day Frank broke his rule forbidding good luck charms other than his knife and took the lighter, buttoned in his tunic pocket. He was hit before even seeing the target and forced to turn back, which he did with relief and disappointment in equal measures.

The target was an airfield beyond Aumale and the weather, with closed cover at 150 feet, was both good and bad. Good because it kept their long approach hidden from German fighters, bad because flying below 150 feet at 340 mph, with visibility of less than half a mile, meant only a split second to spot a target or avoid danger.

Nevertheless, a low-level approach of thirty to forty minutes towards a heavily defended airfield, even if un-harassed by the Luftwaffe, took its toll on each pilot. Isolated in his cockpit, strapped in, hood down, his future was narrowed to the dense, golden, sky-wards rain of 20 mm tracer he was approaching at over 160 yards a second. And between every tracer round there would be all the deadly invisibles, fired from guns bristling like serried rows of dragons' teeth for miles around the target. Crossing those at tree-top height was every pilot's dread, worse than any dog-fight. All knew that for some at least there would be no way through the wall of flak they were hurtling towards, no future beyond it. The rest of life, with its hopes, anticipations, worries and cares, simply fell away, pointless to think about, as blank and unfocused as the camp cinema screen when the projector failed.

Half-way across the Channel the Dodger wriggled his wings, indicating trouble, then executed a wide homeward turn. Frank envied him. No one wanted to do this raid, although no-one wanted not to be part of it. The Dodger had been part and now would live to fight another day. Typical Dodger, having it both ways.

'Turning left now.' Patrick broke radio silence as he rolled and slid beneath Frank, briefly out of sight. They were still ten minutes and thirty seconds from target and would make another turn in three minutes, intended to mislead the Germans as to where they were heading. That was assuming the Germans had located them; with luck, the low cloud, intermittent fog and their low-level approach using hills and woods to shield them from radar would still make for surprise.

Once they were all on the new course, though a few feet higher because the fog in the valleys had thickened, Frank tried to re-enter the daydream he had kept running in the back of his mind since being woken that morning. It was his way of dealing with the approaching flak, that and concentration on details of height, trim, engine revs and location, precisely paralleling Patrick one hundred yards behind and ten yards adrift of his starboard wingtip. He could do this while running a secret mental film of himself digging the colonel's garden, with the colonel out of sight and Vanessa very much in sight and saying something to him. The vision was never particular enough to hear what she was saying but he was forever approaching it.

He was still coming to it when Patrick pulled up sharply to the right. Frank did the same, his mental film instantly dispelled and replaced by a glimpse through the fog of a railway embankment and a goods train loaded with huge tarpaulin-covered shapes on every other bogie. Tanks, no doubt, like the one they had shot up recently. This time no one was in a position to fire but the gun crews must have heard them because the bogies between the tanks lit up and Frank found himself flying through fountains of golden tracer. Instinctively and uselessly, he sank his head between his shoulders. In another instant he was clear and the fountains were all behind him.

A loud metallic bang shook the aircraft and a shock like a kick in the abdomen loosened his grip on the controls, reverberating in his skull. He was rocked by the waves of passing shells and for a few seconds he didn't know how or where he flew, his head ringing and his eyes still dazzled by the strings of tracer. A railway signal box leapt up before him and flashed beneath, then he was in cloud and flying blind.

The engine still ran and responded, there was no smoke, his gauges were normal, the controls worked. He was panting and there was a bitter, unpleasant taste in his mouth. Carefully, he eased off speed and lost height, aiming to get back below the cloud. Once there, he found himself alone above shallow valleys and dreary wet woods and fields, with no other aircraft in sight. For a few more seconds he considered carrying on; with everything working, there was no obvious reason not to, provided he could find the target. But if he did he'd arrive minutes after the attack, with the defences aroused and German fighters probably off the ground by then. And he must surely have sustained damage; he couldn't have taken a hit as violent as that without. Maybe it was his undercarriage, which would prevent him landing. Looking out either side, he saw that the leading edge of his starboard wing was holed like a kitchen cullender.

He turned due west for home.

It was a different sort of loneliness now; the solitary secret thrill of one who got away, his mind free to range beyond the wall of flak rather than fantasise in order to exclude it. He found himself thinking about his father, wondering how he was killed, what his wall had been, whether he had seen it coming or whether it had simply dropped on him from above. For the first time in his life he wondered what he was like, this man who had known even less of him than he of his father; at least he knew he had had a father. He had never felt any different to his step-siblings but now he realised he must be. Feeling he had a future again meant he could indulge in the luxury of a past. He would ask the colonel about this other Frank Foucham's life and death. He might have had a wall, too. Must have, as must the colonel.

The cloud lifted as he approached the Channel. He ascended with it, keeping just in its base and increasing speed. He looked for his navigation point, an automatic flak post on the cliffs near Étretat. Reliably, almost comfortingly, it saluted his passing with a graceful arc of tracer which curved harmlessly down into the dead calm sea behind him. That meant he could turn north towards Beachy Head. Way out in the Channel he passed a solitary French fishing boat whose crew waved a tricolour flag.

Back at the airfield he did two low, slow passes so

that the control tower could check his landing gear. It came down and everything, they said, looked in place. He landed carefully, dipping his port wing to take the strain off the starboard. Inspecting afterwards, the ground crew could find no hole in that wing nor any major damage, except for myriad small perforations and cracks. It looked as if someone had fired a shotgun into it several times at close range.

The engineering officer shrugged. 'Near miss. Probably a 37 mm exploding at the limit of its range. Peppered you a bit.'

Frank couldn't forget the concussing shock. He didn't want anyone to think he had turned back prematurely. 'I can't believe there was no impact.'

The engineering officer clapped him on the shoulder. 'Believe me, old son, if there had been you wouldn't have had a wing and you wouldn't be here now to argue about it. That was a near miss.'

In the mess he found the Dodger alone at the piano, an untouched pint of beer on top of it. He was playing something classical, something soft and melodious. Frank knew nothing of classical music but guessed that this subtle and melancholy piece was difficult to play, unlike the Dodger's usual raucous repertoire. The Dodger was clearly a more gifted pianist than he let on. Alone and unaware of Frank, he played from memory, his broad features softened and abstracted as he gave himself wholly to something beyond himself.

It was a moment of stillness for Frank, which he would have prolonged but for one of the mess staff barging through the door with a crate of bottles. The Dodger broke off and looked round. His abstraction vanished and with it his sensitive, questing intelligence. He left one hand to complete a trite jingle on the keyboard, grinning at Frank.

'What-ho, Moose? You back for an early bath, too? What happened?'

His own turn-back, he said, was due to a mysterious engine malfunction. It would misfire and lose power, then pick up and run normally for a while, then cough and weaken again. 'I suspect a fuel line problem. Seemed OK when I landed, of course. Just didn't fancy my chances in the flak if it went into dawdle on the approach.'

Frank nodded. He was right to turn back. He'd have been a liability to the rest. If they hadn't crashed into him they'd have had to shepherd him home.

'Have a drink,' said the Dodger. 'My call. Tell me about your problem.'

They drank beer and waited for the others. The Dodger downed his rapidly and got another while Frank was still a quarter of the way through his. The Dodger's face was flushed when he sat again, sighing. 'Ever think about what you'll do when the show's over? The whole thing, I mean, the big show, the war. Go back to shooting moose instead of Jerry?'

Frank hadn't. It was a long while since he had thought more than a day – or the next op – ahead.

'You could go crop-spraying,' said the Dodger. 'Plenty of scope in Canada. Plenty of practice, too, with all this low-level stuff we do.'

'I guess so. Or run a flying-boat service.' Most likely he would go back and finish his engineering degree, and then see. 'You?'

'No idea. My old man's a bank manager, wanted me to go into it. Partly why I'm here. To be honest, I can't imagine a future. Too knackered after this.'

'Be a concert pianist. Sounds as if you could.'

The Dodger stared into his beer, shaking his head. 'Could have, maybe. Not now. Don't have the application. Lost it.'

'Didn't sound like that to me.'

'That's 'cos you know bugger all about music.'

At the sound of a plane coming in they went to the window. The runway was out of sight of the mess but they could see planes as they taxied back. The first was Davy Jones's, a garrulous Welshman from Cardiff.

'Trust him to be first back,' said the Dodger. 'Last in, first out, that's his game.' He sounded uncharacteristically bitter.

'You reckon?'

'Always. Haven't you noticed?'

They counted them in during the next quarter-hour

or so. It was obvious even from a distance that several had been damaged, one with a fire-blackened fuselage. Patrick was last in. They were one short, another new boy called Ian something.

'Usually the new ones,' said the Dodger. 'Old ones like us know the dodges. We're all dodgers if we last six months.'

'He may have ditched or landed somewhere.'

'Keep saying it.'

The mess was lively again that night. The raid was judged a success because fuel and ammunition dumps had been hit, though photo-reconnaissance had yet to confirm how many planes had been destroyed. Everyone seemed in a mood to forget the war for an hour or two and no one mentioned Ian, who was posted missing. His aircraft was reported during the debrief to have been hit by flak but not too badly, trailing a thin stream of oil smoke as he pulled up and away. They all lost each other in the cloud but when they loosely regrouped over the Channel Ian did not reappear. German fighters were by then airborne and it was thought he might have fallen prey to them. It was still possible he might have bailed out and been captured.

'Better than bailing out over Germany,' someone said. There were tales of bomber crews being beaten or murdered by angry civilians.

During a shouted conversation at the bar, which

both only half-heard, Frank told Patrick about the colonel and Vanessa and about the invitation to bring some of the boys round. 'I was thinking maybe if just you and I go, make sure it's OK. Then we can take some others another time.' He wasn't sure why he was doing it. Partly, he suspected, because he wanted to show off to Patrick and partly because he thought Vanessa would be impressed. Not that he wanted to share her in any way, even if she had been his to share. Partly also because he felt they wanted him to bring a few of the boys round, to help them feel they were doing their bit for the war.

Patrick, who normally drank sparingly, was a few pints away that night. He listened with one hand cupped behind his ear, nodding. 'Good idea,' he shouted. 'Not tonight.'

'No, not tonight,' shouted Frank.

Chapter Eight

'He was killed outside Lens in early September, 1918,' said the colonel. 'I was with him.'

The blackout curtains were drawn and the dining room was mostly in shadow. Feeble yellow light from the two table lamps just encompassed the four empty plates but only Frank and the colonel remained at the table, sharing an ashtray, their glasses refilled. Vanessa and Patrick were in the drawing room across the hall, playing jazz on the gramophone and dancing. Vanessa had suggested it when they finished dinner.

'Shall we dance?' she asked, smiling across the table at Patrick. 'Now, before coffee? What passes for coffee. Leave these two to their war talk.'

The light caught her eyes, making them sparkle. Frank felt it like a knife twisted in his breast. Patrick put down his glass and stood, smiling back at her. 'My pleasure, madam.'

Now, the music had stopped. Perhaps they were changing records. Frank hoped so. To think they might be doing anything else – embracing – was unbearable. The colonel was relighting his pipe with Frank Foucham's lighter, which Frank had pushed across the table to him. He wanted to hear what the colonel had to say, although it was hard to pay attention.

'What happened?' he asked, belatedly. The music started again as he spoke. That was something.

'You may think it odd he should have been with us, The Royal West Kents, not a Canadian regiment. We were a Kitchener battalion, you see, and he'd been in the Territorial battalion with me before the war, before his father sent him to Canada. When he came back with his Canadian lot he somehow got dispensation to be attached to us on temporary transfer. He'd been promoted by the Canadians and was senior to me but I was jolly pleased when he took over the company to which I was sent as a platoon commander. Rather elderly platoon commander, I'm afraid – I was older than him. He was pleased too, I hope. It was good to be together again. Good for me, anyway.'

Frank hated to picture them dancing but couldn't stop himself. He held out his hand for the lighter. 'So how was he killed?'

'Well, that's rather a long story, I'm afraid. Not what happened on the day, of course – it was quick enough, mercifully – but how it came about.'

The music was faster now. He imagined them jitterbugging or something. He was still staring at the cigarette between his fingers, ignored after the first drag, when he realised that the colonel was waiting for him to say something. He met his rheumy eyes. 'Sure, I'd like to hear it, the whole thing, if you've time. How it came about. What happened.'

'She happened. Maud. It began with her.' The colonel nodded at the portrait over the fireplace of the woman in the garden. Her face was in shadow but her white dress stood out. 'She was a village girl, here, from the cottages up the track by the pub, just off the green. Her parents were not local. They were both in service and they wanted to carry on and so her mother gave her as a baby to her two sisters who had married two brothers, woodmen. They all lived in those cottages and one of the sisters brought her up with her own daughter. She went to school here and then into service with the Dudley Gordons over at Penshurst, the other side of Tonbridge. They're part of the De L'Isle family at Penshurst Place and lived nearby at Swaylands. She did very well, worked for both families, got on. She was beautiful, as you can see, but clever, too. People liked her. Despite her rebellious streak.' He smiled. 'Got up the nose of Hilary Wooding, Johnny Wooding's snob of a wife, for refusing to curtsey to her. Hilary fancied herself the squire's wife, you see, though Johnny had no real claim to be squire, and, to be fair, didn't make one. If any family here did, it would be mine, I suppose. Me, now.' He shook his head, still smiling. 'Anyway, Maud did well in service, got promoted to the nursery and went with the Dudley Gordons to Phoenix Park in Dublin when the Earl was viceroy. Before the war, of course.'

The music stopped again. Frank waited. Again, he realised the colonel was waiting for him. 'What happened?'

'In Dublin she lived in the vice-regal lodge, had charge of the offspring, including the heir whom I believe is a guardsman now, doing very well apparently. Used to take him in his pram in Phoenix Park, always in a hat and long gloves and with a policeman escorting her. Got a photo somewhere. Different world now.' He sipped his wine. 'After that, back here, what happened was that she met Frank, your father. He began courting her, as we used to say then. That's what caused all the trouble. You see, his people – your people, your ancestors – were yeomen stock, not a county family but prosperous independent farmers, as I was saying before. Well-respected, known in hunting and shooting circles. In other words, a few rungs up the ladder from a penniless village girl.'

Frank nodded. Again, he didn't correct the colonel on his parentage, letting the old man run on. It did no harm. The music had resumed. It was tedious listening to this rigmarole about this other Frank

Foucham's girlfriend from pre-history while his mind was with Vanessa and Patrick across the hall. He tried to look attentive.

It seemed to work. The colonel nodded as if Frank had spoken. 'Well, once it got out that they were seeing each other, both families were unhappy, his because she was not at all the match his people wanted for him, hers because she was getting above herself, as they saw it. So they began to meet in secret, by the Medway, sometimes in a hired boat. Whenever she had time off she'd walk the seven or so miles into Tonbridge, which they did for shopping anyway, and he'd take a pony and trap from here. With me as cover. We were friends, you see.

'That was a bit awkward, too, as far as my people were concerned. We lived here in the manor, I'd been sent away to school and so on, whereas they were just local farmers and Frank spoke with a Kentish accent. But we'd grown up together, shot, fished and hunted together, even the odd spot of poaching for the fun of it. Only from unpopular landowners – well, one actually, Johnny Wooding. We liked each other, respected each other – at least, I respected him. He was better at everything than me – better shot, better rider, better poacher even. But that didn't matter. We were friends.

'So he and I would take old Bluebell in the trap to the Medway, ostensibly to go fishing. I actually did fish, while he went off in the boat for his trysts with

Maud.' The colonel again held out his hand for the lighter and relit his pipe. 'I think I can honestly say I wasn't jealous. Envious, yes, enormously, but not jealous. It seemed appropriate that he rather than me should have her. He was the better man. I didn't begrudge him; I admired him. Anyway, with war coming – we all felt it was, you see, felt it in our bones – we joined the Territorials, me with a commission because I'd been in the cadets at school, Frank as an OR. Again, it didn't make any difference to us.

'What did, though, was his father finding out he was still seeing Maud. We never knew how – presumably someone saw them – but the result was that Frank was sent to Canada to help his brother, who was there already, farm some land the old man had bought. I think I told you. Land in Canada was cheap then and old George Foucham had amassed a pretty penny through his farming and butchery business. So they were broken up, Frank and Maud. Before he left he gave her a ring as a keepsake, a plain silver band he made from a teaspoon – he was pretty handy like that, another difference between us – and promised he'd be in touch. It was probably all he could manage without his parents knowing.

'Anyway, he went and she waited and waited and didn't hear. War came and I was mobilised with the Territorials and after a while posted to the Eighth Battalion, one of many new Kitchener battalions, to help train them. Not that I had any idea what we were in for, no more than anyone else. Meanwhile, I had started seeing Maud myself. Not courting at that stage, but seeing her. It came about when I ran into her by chance one day in Tonbridge, near the station, and she asked if I'd heard from Frank. I hadn't but hoped to sometime and said I'd let her know if I did. She usually had to go shopping on Saturdays and we arranged to meet in the station buffet at 1130 whenever I could get in. I could often get away at weekends, you see. We were pretty sure we wouldn't meet anyone either of us knew there on a Saturday.

'Of course, I was in love with her. Had been since the day I met her. But I don't think I acknowledged it then, even to myself, let alone her. She was Frank's girl and he would come back for her, I was sure of that. But I loved seeing her, talking to her, being with her. Our teas became walks by the river and in the intervals I would think of things to tell her, questions to ask about her own life. I knew the family she worked for, you see, and although she was loyal, fiercely loyal, it was interesting to hear about life below stairs. But we also talked about books. She had only a village education but she was a keen reader. I'd talk about a book – Dickens or whatever, she venerated Dickens – and by next time she'd have read it if she could find it, borrowing from her employers or the library. I started giving her books and she built up her own library. Our talks were the beginnings of her education, she told me later. That wasn't how I saw them. I think I assumed they were a distraction from her unhappiness about not hearing from Frank and she, I thought, saw contact with me as a remote way of keeping in touch with him. It suited both of us. It never occurred to me then that she and I could have any sort of future. At least, I didn't dare think of it.

'Then I was sent away and saw less of her, but since most of our training was on the Downs near Shoreham and around Surrey or Aldershot, I could get back now and again. Neither of us heard from Frank. I would call on his people and they'd say all was going well with both brothers, that the farm was coming on and so on, but never anything personal.

'Then we entrained for France and the debacle of Loos, our introduction to war. Lost almost all my friends. We had leave afterwards while the battalion re-formed. Seven days' home leave. I'd get only another ten in the next three years, though fortunately I didn't know it at the time. It was odd, I couldn't settle; grateful to be home but restless. I saw Maud only once during that week. Don't mind me telling you all this personal stuff, do you? Don't usually talk about it.' His bushy white eyebrows were raised.

'Not at all, sir, I'm very interested.' It was different music now, slower, waltzy stuff. They were probably dancing toe to toe, holding each other close.

'I proposed to her. We were walking by the Medway. I hadn't intended to – maybe there's something about walking by water. I think I was also more shaken by Loos than I realised. I was going back three days afterwards and probably thought I'd never see her again. It didn't make sense from any rational or practical point of view but the heart has its own seasons, they say.' He slowly turned the lighter over and over in his hand. 'Maybe it was also, sub-consciously, a way of staking a claim on the future, acting as if there was one, even though I didn't believe it. Maybe that's why she said yes, too. It just came out, you see. We'd been talking about the gardens at Swaylands, of which Lady Dudley Gordon was doing some rather fine water colours, and there was a pause, and I heard myself say, "I love you, Maud, and what I've been wanting to say all this time is, will you marry me?" It just came out. My voice broke as I said "I love you". I didn't say anything else. I just stopped walking and looked at her. I was so surprised I'd said it. I think she was too.'

The colonel paused. The music went on. The pause was long enough for Frank to feel it was time he asked what happened next, when the colonel resumed.

'She looked at me and said, "Yes." That was all, for a while. We just stared at each other. Then she said, "I must tell Frank." I said, "Would you like me to?" She said, "No, it must come from me." Then we linked arms and continued our walk.' He smiled. 'Very tame by modern standards.'

'What happened next?'

'Anyway, I got Frank's address from his family and Maud wrote and told him. For a while she didn't hear – actually, we were married by the time she did, which meant another seven days' leave for me. My people weren't happy about it, of course, but the war produced a rash of hasty marriages and they were so worried they might never see me again that they went along with anything I wanted. When your father did reply it was heart-breaking, even for me. It made me feel worse, though I never regretted marrying Maud. I was deliriously happy. That never changed. I just hope she felt the same.'

There was another pause.

'Frank, your father, had ridden forty miles on horseback to pick up the letter at the nearest post. He hadn't written before, he said, because he didn't want to until he could say, come and join me, the farm is ready, I've built the house, let's start a new life. That plain silver band he made was meant as an engagement ring, only he never told her. God knows what she really felt. She didn't say at the time – I was in France – and she showed me the letter only after he was killed.

'Anyway, Frank joined the Canadian Army shortly after getting her letter and was soon commissioned, rightly. I don't know whether he met and married your mother before he joined or after but it must have been about the same time. I don't know whether she even knows about Maud. Has she ever . . . ?'

This time he couldn't let it go. 'Like I said before, sir, it wasn't him my mother married but another Foucham, Francis W. Foucham.'

It made no difference. The old man went on as if Frank hadn't spoken. 'Some time later – after you were conceived, obviously – he was sent to England for further training before France. It was then that he applied for secondment to his old regiment. That was accepted and he was posted to us in the line to take over D company, there being yet another vacancy. I had no idea of this until one night when we were in support I was sent from A company to take over as second-in-command D company, which was in the line. Another vacancy. Neither of us expected to see the other there, me because I'd no idea he'd come over from Canada, him because he assumed I was still with our old Territorial battalion.

'This was in the midst of Operation Michael, the German Spring Offensive of March 1918, their last throw before they collapsed in the autumn. Things were pretty desperate, we were falling back, falling back night and day and pretty soon we were back in trenches we'd taken in 1916. Exhausting, confusing and dispiriting, especially when we'd make a stand, hold our position and then had to abandon it because the units on either side gave way or were wiped out. We did better than most, partly because we were one of the first to adopt defence in depth – just one company forward with the rest deployed farther back so that we weren't all obliterated by the initial assault. That was what happened when you held the line in strength, with all companies forward and just one in support. The first intense barrage combined with the initial shock troops cut swathes through the forward positions and then you had nothing behind to stop them when they broke through.

'It was a wet night when I reported to D company dugout, rain like stair rods and mud you just can't imagine until you've been in it. It took me nearly two hours to cover about three quarters of a mile, in full kit, of course, slipping, sliding, soaking, getting stuck, getting un-stuck, wrong turns, collapsed trenches, all in pitch dark. There wasn't much going on, fortunately – the odd shell or nervous machine-gunner – but it wouldn't have made much difference if there had been. It was the elements, the elements and conditions that were the worst thing for most of us. You arrive cold, wet, tired and hungry. You don't start your battles fresh, you're on your knees. People don't realise.

'When eventually I reached A company and was directed to company headquarters someone mentioned Captain Foucham but I was too exhausted and dulled to take it in, just thought I'd misheard. I knew his predecessor had been killed and that there was a replacement but didn't know who. The dugout – really just a hollowed-out bit of trench with a canvas flap – was lit by a single candle on a table made of ammunition boxes. Seated on another ammunition box, hatless, tunic unbuttoned, smoking and looking at an old trench map, was your father.

Frank held up his hand, shaking his head, but said nothing. Maybe it was shell-shock from the last war.

The colonel didn't appear to have noticed his gesture. 'I saw immediately that it was him but it was a few seconds before he recognised me in my helmet and with all my clobber and covered in mud. We just stared at each other without speaking and now for the life of me I can't remember who was the first to speak or who said what. Funny isn't it, eh?' The colonel smiled. 'I know we shook hands and each said something about what a surprise and not expecting to see the other and each gave an account of how we came to be there. Of course, there was a third person in the dugout – Maud – but neither of us mentioned her. In moments of great surprise or shock we reach for the ordinary, don't we? The banal, the everyday, the practical, the obvious. That's what you cling to while you re-adjust.

'And then there really was someone else in the dugout, Hobbs, the company runner. And then briefing and introductions and finding somewhere to dump my kit and everything else and in no time you're immersed in mundanity, the endless mundanities of trench life, or family life or working life or whatever you're doing, the Duke of Wellington's one-damn-thing-after-another of it all that fills our hours and prevents us thinking about where we're going. Just as well, perhaps.'

Seeing Frank take out another cigarette, the colonel pushed the lighter across to him. There had been no music for a while now. Frank imagined them talking to each other, becoming intimate.

'We never did talk about it, the obvious subject. There was never time for the personal, too much going on, and when you weren't busy you were sleeping, or trying to. We were never alone, anyway, apart from the odd half-minute. But there was an unspoken understanding that sometime we would. And we were not estranged. We simply resumed from where we left off before he went to Canada, as if we were on an extended poaching expedition on old Johnny Wooding's land. We made a good team, your father and I, always did. Knew each other so well we didn't need to explain. But that was also what worried me, you see, more than the Maud business. I sensed he knew my secret and I was terrified it would come out. As it did, very soon it did.'

He paused again, looking at Frank as if expecting him to know. 'Your secret?' Frank asked.

'My fear. My secret fear.'

There was another pause. 'But everyone's afraid, aren't they, sir? I am. I'm sure all the guys are, every time we go up.'

'Of course, of course, you take that for granted and get on with your job. So long as you keep going, just do your job and keep going, you'll be all right. There were cases of shell-shock but they were understood and accepted, couldn't be helped. What I'm talking about is another level of fear. Incapacitating fear, when you're paralysed, lose control of your body, want to go on but your legs won't move. It hadn't happened to me by then but I knew it would, I'd seen it in others and I knew it would come to me one day. And that made me more afraid, afraid of my own fear. That was my secret and I lived in a perpetual funk because of it.'

'I know what you mean.' Frank surprised himself. It came out so easily. He heard himself saying it without having intended it, like the colonel's proposal.

'You do?' The colonel stared. It was impossible to tell whether he was recalling his own feelings or assessing Frank's. 'When it started I thought it was shell-shock at first. It was following the retreat from Vadencourt – withdrawal, I should say, a fighting withdrawal, the Eighth Battalion never broke, not once. First symptom was the shakes. Nothing unusual about that, most of us did at some time or other. It was just like when you get an eyelid that goes on the blink, you get this trembling in your vision and think everyone else can see it, but they don't. But with me there was something else. I couldn't make myself stand upright, even when I knew it was safe. I crouched all the time and flinched at the slightest noise or unexpected movement. Embarrassing, you just hope no one else will notice. Then one day Frank asked me to lead a raiding party that night across to the German lines to nab a Hun prisoner or two. Not his idea – came down from Brigade via Battalion HQ. They wanted live evidence for their theory – hope – that the offensive was running out of steam, that the Germans were pretty well as exhausted as we were and wouldn't be able to maintain momentum much longer. They were right, as it turned out.

'Not that he asked me directly. It was just after stand-to – you know, that dreadful hour before dawn when you're at your lowest ebb and everyone has to rouse themselves to be ready for a dawn attack which hardly ever comes. I was on the fire-step in number one platoon's position, crouching of course, though I could just see into no-man's-land through some nettles and churned-up earth. Unknown to me, Frank came along the trench behind me, inspecting positions. He put his hand on my shoulder and I winced and shrunk myself, my head between my knees, immediately, uncontrollably.

'"It's all right, it's only me," he whispered.

'When I opened my eyes I saw he was smiling but in a kind way, not mocking as it might have been. Because I know what he saw: a frightened, furtive little animal, paralysed by fear from a mere touch on the shoulder.

'He put his hand on my shoulder again. "It's all right, Ken, it's all right, don't worry." He spoke as if to a child or pet. "I wanted your advice about something. Come and see me when we stand down."

'Well, it turned out he wanted me to recommend someone to lead the raid. It was to be an all-volunteer job, like most of our raids, and he wanted to let the best candidates know first. Neither of us knew the company well, of course. When I said I would do it he looked at me for a long moment, the candlelight flickering on one side of his face. It was not just Maud who was our unacknowledged companion now but that frightened little animal. "Are you sure?" he asked.

'"I want to," I lied. In a way I did, I wanted to show him I was more than just that little animal. I also thought I was going to die anyway so better get it over with before the extent of my funk was discovered. The only other surviving platoon commander was pretty badly knocked up, having been in the front line longer than I had, and it wasn't fair to ask yet more of him. He was killed the following day, as it happened. Trench mortar.

'So I led the patrol out that night. Eight of us, all volunteers, divided into two snatch parties and with Sergeant White as my second-in-command. We didn't have to cut holes in the wire – there wasn't any to speak of by then, retreat being so fluid. We just crawled out in two parallel groups, close enough to communicate.

'We didn't know how far we had to go, of course, because we had only a rough idea where the Hun were and the ground at night is always very different to the topography you think you remember from the day. The odd flare or star shell went up from both sides and then we had to freeze, face down in the mud. You feel so hideously exposed in the glare which seems to last for ages. My buttocks quivered so much I was afraid they might be visible to the enemy.' The colonel laughed and coughed. 'Curiously, I didn't feel frightened just then. Tense, of course, anxious, but concentrated on getting the job done. I'd left my fear behind. Or so I thought.

'When the last flare was fading I made myself raise my head a fraction. I saw the outline of a helmet about thirty yards ahead. It didn't move and could have been a corpse but it looked upright and we knew there was a network of old supply trenches in that area. When the flare had died completely I crawled over to where I reckoned Sergeant White must be and tapped him on the leg. Turned out not to be his leg and not a living one, either. But I found him soon after – or, rather, he found me. I'd unknowingly crawled ahead of him and he grabbed my foot, which was a bit of a shock. Thought it was the dead chap at first.' The colonel's laugh mutated into coughing again. 'Anyhow, we agreed to carry on forward until one of us saw something close enough, in which case he'd shout "Now!" and we'd all get up and rush them. I crawled back to my team and passed the word that it was likely to be soon.

'It was less than another minute. They must have heard or seen something because they opened up with rifles, machine-guns and flares, luckily a bit to our right. I think we all shouted "Now!" Thereafter it was a daze of lights, bangs, tracer, shouts and screams, plus a few crumps as our Mills bombs got into their trench and a lot of stuff in reply which fortunately went over our heads because we'd got amongst them by then.

'Raids are very short-lived, very confusing. Every man comes back with a different story even though they were only feet apart. Same with your dog-fights, I imagine. Anyway, this was a success. We all got back and we nabbed two Huns. Lucky devils, they'd be out of it soon. All except me, that is. Every man got back except me.'

'You were captured? Injured?'

'Still in my hole, in a funk. Couldn't move, you

see. I shouted "Now!" with the others and went to get up but my legs wouldn't move, I just couldn't make myself. It wasn't that I couldn't feel them, as if I was paralysed, I just couldn't make myself do it. It was all going on around me in the dark, people running past shouting, flashes and shots, then running back towards our lines, lots of random fire by then, flares going up, and I just lay there willing myself to move and utterly impotent. No one saw me, they didn't know I wasn't amongst them until they got back.'

'So how did you get back?'

The colonel held out his hand for the lighter, tamped down his pipe, relit it and sipped his wine. 'Courage is keeping going, that's the essence. Not doing anything special or daring, though it includes acts of valour and self-sacrifice. It's putting one foot in front of the other when everything in your body is telling you not to, or when you feel so weak and weary you just want to give up. Same in civilian life: it takes courage sometimes just to go on with the ordinary. In a sense, it's easier in war because it's more defined. For me, as I suspect for most soldiers, it was waiting to go over the top that really took it out of you. Once you were up and over you were caught up in the mayhem, like a maul in a rugby match. You play rugby? Well, like British Bulldog, then. Play that in the mess, don't you?

'But the worst bit was the waiting, knowing it was going to happen, looking at your watch and counting down to the whistle, feeling empty in your stomach and not knowing whether your legs would move when ordered. That's the hardest thing, you see, being in the front line of the infantry when ordered to advance into fire. It's the essence of infantry work, what you have to do to win battles, but nothing in land war is more frightening or more dangerous. Your equivalent of low-level attacks into flak.'

'You've heard about them, I guess, sir?'

'Another thing about courage is that it's finite. Like energy, it gets used up. You only have so much. I was already living on a courage overdraft when I went to ground that night and somehow, in that little hollow, I reached my overdraft limit. When I went to get up, there was nothing left.'

There was another silence. The colonel's pauses made it difficult to tell whether he was waiting to resume or waiting for a response, or had simply ceased to be aware of his listener. There was still no more music but in the silence Frank heard Vanessa laugh, another twist of the knife. 'But you got back?' he persisted.

'Frank got me back. They realised I was missing, of course, didn't know whether dead or injured but Sergeant White knew roughly where I'd gone to ground. He offered to go out again but Frank insisted and crawled out himself. It was more dangerous then than when we'd gone out the first time because the enemy was thoroughly alerted. I was still in my funk hole, didn't know what to do, hadn't moved an inch, when I heard movement behind me, realised it must be someone from our own lines. Strangely, that did it – I found I could move again. I'd just started to slither round when he found me. We were both lying down, face to face. "You all right?" he whispered.

'"Fine," I said, "I'm sorry."

'He patted me on the helmet. "Don't be."

'"I funked it. Couldn't move. I'm so sorry."

'"Follow me."

'When we got back to our trench I heard him say to Sergeant White, "Concussion. Be OK when he's had a rest. I'll send him back to Battalion HQ with the prisoners, detail two men to go as guards."

'Back in the dugout I tried to explain to Frank again but he cut me short. "Forget it, these things happen. Main thing now is to get the prisoners back quickly so they can get them to Brigade for interrogation. No need to hurry back. That's probably all the action we're getting for the night. Get some sleep somewhere."

'That was the last I saw of him. We delivered the two prisoners after the usual mishaps of trench travel at night, nearly getting shot by our own HQ company sentries. I had a feeling he intended me to stay out of the line and be rested and was perhaps sending a separate message to the CO to that effect, so I didn't hang around to hear it but set off back again with the two guards. Not that I wanted to go back, of course, but I couldn't bear to feel I'd let Frank down. Especially as I'd married Maud.'

'What happened to him?'

'Strange thing about guilt is that you can become possessive about it, hoarding it, treasuring it because it makes you feel special. You, uniquely among all humanity, bear this burden. It's corrosive, like too much grief, turning you inwards on yourself rather than outwards towards others. In the end I had no relief until I told Maud everything. She had known and loved him and if she could forgive me, I reckoned, then I could begin to accept myself. Frank was the love of her life, you see, never me. But I accepted that, too.'

'When was he killed?'

'He was wrong about the rest of the night being quiet. They punished us for the raid with a bout of shelling. The company HQ dugout, where Frank would normally have been, was untouched but he'd remained in the section of trench where we'd come back and it was that corner that was hit. Him and Sergeant White. I got back to find myself in charge of the company. Ironic, eh?'

'So it wasn't your fault? You didn't need to feel too guilty?'

'Chance that he'd stayed there, yes, but he wouldn't have been there at all if he hadn't rescued me. His body wasn't – it wasn't a direct hit. The shell landed just behind, collapsing the trench wall even though it was a dud, didn't go off. Neither he nor Sergeant White had a mark on them. It must have passed very close and the over-pressure burst their lungs, or the vacuum collapsed them. Better way to go than most, I guess. I shouldn't have kept this' – he touched the lighter with his fingertip – 'but I wanted something to remember him by and doubted his next of kin would have any use for it. Pleased to be proved wrong after all this time.' He smiled at Frank as he got up, with obvious effort. 'Bladder calls. One of the crosses of age. Don't get old, Frank.'

He shuffled towards the door. He was old, thought Frank, old before his time. He might only be in his fifties but he looked ten years older. Perhaps it was the wine. Frank remained seated, his fingers curled round his wine glass. Listening to the colonel's story, he had neglected to drink and now, listening to the silence from the drawing room across the hall, he neglected the story. Were they choosing more music, kneeling together on the floor? Were they on the sofa with each other, talking quietly and intimately in what he imagined to be the preliminary to mutual seduction? He couldn't bring himself to blame her; Patrick was everything he assumed a woman would want. He didn't blame Patrick, either. He was jealous of her attention going elsewhere but not of Patrick himself. They were right for each other, they deserved each other, like the colonel's Frank and his Maud. He was envious, that was all, envious that it happened to others, not to him.

The door opened. 'Come on, what are you sitting here for? Come and dance.' She was flushed and smiling, her outstretched bare arm resting on the door handle.

Patrick appeared behind her. 'Better not give the Moose ideas. Time we got moving. May have a busy day tomorrow.'

Frank stood, picking up the lighter. 'Sorry, we've been talking.'

She folded her arms. 'War talk, I suppose?'

'The last war.'

'Makes a change. Next time we dance. Promise?'

Pleased, he nodded and smiled. 'Sure thing.'

The back tyre of Patrick's bike was flat. They pumped it but it wouldn't hold air, so they had to push the bikes back to base. It was almost an hour's walk and very dark except for the sky to the south-east which was punctured by flashes accompanied by the crump of bombs and bark of ack-ack.

'Dover or Folkestone getting a pasting,' said Patrick. 'Probably by the Yanks, getting the wrong side of the Channel.'

For a few seconds the memory of Tony walked with them. Frank realised he was forgetting him already.

'Seems a nice old boy,' said Patrick. 'Knows his wine. Generous with it, too.'

'He's convinced himself he knew my father, my real father, in the last war and that he was with him just before he was killed. He didn't and he wasn't, same name, different man. But he won't listen when I tell him. Not sure he's right in the head.'

'Well, that's something to write home about. War throws up extraordinary coincidences. I knew a chap who ditched in the North Sea and was picked up by his own brother, who was in the Navy.'

The flashes and crumps died away, leaving only the sounds of their boots and wheels on the lane. Patrick was leading, a moving solid patch of dark. Frank was longing to ask about Vanessa. 'Have you got any puncture repair kit?' he asked instead.

'No, but someone will. If we can glue planes back together there'll be something to glue a bike tyre.'

'Have a good dance?'

'Very good, yes, ages since I had a dance. Bit odd capering about in boots, but still. Don't think I damaged her too badly. You should've joined in. She thought perhaps you didn't like dancing.'

'Colonel kept me talking.'

Chapter Nine

No one in the squadron knew the date or location of the D-Day landings but everyone knew they were imminent. Operational tempo increased, with sweeps and sorties over northern France and attacks on trains and marshalling yards. They escorted Typhoons on tree-top attacks against heavily-defended airfields, grateful that their role involved dog-fights with the Luftwaffe rather than flying head-on into flak. The Typhoons continued to pay a heavy price and even when every Spitfire in the squadron returned unscathed the mood was subdued.

They were subdued in advance, however, when ordered to escort 130 Flying Fortresses on an attack on the marshalling yards of Rouen. Not only because of their recent experience of American trigger-happiness and poor recognition skills but because being close escort meant flying too slowly to respond quickly to an attack. Their fellow squadron was luckier, escorting from above and behind.

'Trust us to get the bloody close escort,' said the Dodger as they left the briefing.

'Look upon it as an honour,' said Patrick. 'And shut up.'

He was uncharacteristically tetchy that day, perhaps a symptom of the tiredness that afflicted them all. Repeated sorties, sometimes several a day, with their inevitable losses – not great but regular enough – exacted a toll on energy and optimism. When the MO, their gruffly cheerful Scottish doctor, handed out extra Benzedrine, Frank was one of the first to take some. Despite eating everything that came his way, he was losing weight and the intermittent nervous tic in his left eyelid had returned. He had not had it since his first operational week on the squadron. It felt as if it must be obvious to everyone but, as the colonel had said, it usually wasn't. Curiously, the occasional trembling in his arms and legs, which reminded him of what the colonel had said about his own involuntary flinching and crouching, became less frequent as he became more tired. His reflexes were still sharp, he was doing everything he should, but he was doing it mechanically, without that extra edge of awareness he knew made the difference. He managed each take-off in a state of suspended reality, a combination of his old familiar, his stomach-tightening fear, and careless, light-headed fatigue. Complacency, disguised as fatalism, was seeping into him. He knew it and did nothing about it, assuming it was the same for everyone.

'D'you feel honoured?' asked the Dodger when they were in the Dispersal hut and Patrick was out of earshot. 'Buggered if I do. Bloody stupid idea if ever I heard one. What does he think we are – boy scouts?' He had just loaded and holstered his revolver and was now cramming his pockets with ammunition.

'What do you want with all that?' Frank asked. 'Taking pot-shots at ME110s as they pass us?'

The new German jets were making their presence felt and the Allies, having neglected to develop the British invention, had no answer to them.

'In case I'm shot down. Same with any of us. You never know, do you? Not much use with just six in the chamber. Hell of a lot of Germans over there. I take an extra pistol, too.'

'How? Where?'

'Jam it down by my seat.'

It was a bad sign. Pilots who took ever more elaborate precautions against being shot down often were, not long afterwards. Patrick's theory was that their minds were no longer wholly on their jobs. 'Better off keeping sharp on your cannon,' he would say. 'More likely you'll come back.'

The exchange with the Dodger helped Frank take his mind off himself. As they lined up three abreast on the runway, waiting for the signal, engines roaring and props a blur, he decided he wouldn't take the Dodger to meet the colonel and Vanessa.

The 130 Flying Fortresses were prompt at their rendezvous, filling half the sky with their immaculate defensive boxes. That was all very well but the big bombers were no wave-topping Typhoons and would cross the Channel smack in the middle of German radar coverage. Patrick led the squadron carefully alongside them, approaching from far out and keeping rigorously parallel so that there was no excuse for the Fortress gunners to mistake them for a threat. Even so, one let off a brief stream of tracer towards the Dodger's Spitfire, fortunately at the limit of his range and well behind the Dodger. Frank, juggling with engine revs and speed as he tried to keep one high enough to react and the other low enough to stay with their charges, did not at first see the lifting of the Dodger's starboard wing as he began a turn towards the offending Fortress, lining up his cannon.

Patrick broke radio silence. 'Cut it, Dodger! Stow it! Get back in formation.'

The Dodger's port wing dipped and he re-aligned himself.

They were very soon on the run-in to Rouen.

Surprisingly, there were no fighters but the flak was as expected over a railway town, tracer curving in graceful overlapping arcs like ribbons of welcome. The escorting Spitfires moved up and back, leaving the bombers to the flak and their task. There was little cloud, so they had a perfect view of what happened. The marshalling yards were on the far bank of the winding Seine, spreading wide and clear to the north in the morning sun. Before them, on the near side of the river and well to the south, the reddish roofs of the town clustered around the cathedral spire. The Fortresses were in the final minute of their run-in, lined up in perfect bombing formation. As they closed, the flak intensified, though no worse than usual. No planes went down, no engines plumed black smoke, no wings lit up. Then the lead bombardier lost his nerve; at least, that was the only explanation they could all agree on afterwards.

At his command, 130 Fortresses unloaded over the town, still well south of the marshalling yards and on the wrong side of the river. Within seconds the crowded little red roofs were peppered by flashes and flame. Within a few more they were obscured by smoke billowing upwards, great tumbling black clouds punctured by ever more flashes and spurts of flame from below. For one moment, as Frank wheeled in disbelief, he glimpsed the cathedral spire standing alone amidst the conflagration. The empty bombers turned over the untouched marshalling yards, reforming.

At first, all the close escort Spitfires wheeled, like Frank, in shocked disbelief, eyes on the carnage below rather than scanning the skies for the Luftwaffe. Radio silence was broken by the Dodger.

'The bastards! The murdering bastards!' he shouted. 'Murdering bloody Yanks!'

Others joined in, a cacophony of invective. Frank said nothing. He could only wheel and watch, stunned into silence. The Dodger and another had already turned their planes towards the re-forming Fortresses when Patrick called them to order, the only calm voice amidst the outrage. 'Button it everybody. Save your ammo for the Luftwaffe. Re-form close escort.'

They returned without incident. There was much talk afterwards about how it could have happened and how, if a Fortress had let off a single mistaken round at the escort, they would have brought it down. The outrage quickly spread across the entire base, transmuting itself into a rowdy mess night during which someone put planks up to the windows and rode a motorbike in and along the horseshoe of tables. The wing commander's dinner ended up in his lap, along with bits of broken plate, and the motorcyclist broke his leg when a table toppled and he came off. This was followed by British Bulldog. They all knew that the cost of replacing mess furniture would appear on their mess bills.

'Only if we live long enough to get them,' said the Dodger.

He was uncharacteristically quiet that night, avoiding the rumpus and not even doing a turn on the piano. He sat drinking with Frank and a few other refugees in armchairs in the bar, trying to ignore the shouting, laughter and occasional sounds of breaking glass.

'Bet they deduct it from the pay they owe you before it goes to next of kin,' the Dodger continued. He took a swig of his beer and turned to Frank. 'You've left everything to your folks back home, I suppose?'

'What there is.' They'd all had to make wills.

'Quite. You don't make much out of this man's war, that's for sure. Unless you're a Yank.'

There was no point in going to bed early because the revellers would wake everyone when they returned to the huts. There was some desultory talk of life after the war, a recurring subject when there was nothing else that anyone wanted to talk about and which, being safely remote, didn't involve any commitment. Anything seemed possible, nothing likely.

'Of course, the problem's going to be the population,' said the Dodger.

'Which population?'

'Everyone's, all of it, the world's. Too many people, that's going to be the problem.'

'Guess we need the war to go on, then.'

The Dodger laughed and raised his glass. 'I'll drink to that.'

There was no flying the next day, with fog and low cloud grounding everything. Despite this, they weren't released from standby until the afternoon. Frank decided to go fishing, although there were likely to be as few fish rising as planes flying. He didn't tell anyone he was going.

For a long time he stood in the wet grass, casting and re-casting between the willows. The river was sluggish and no fish were tempted by his wet fly. He didn't much mind. It was soothing to fish without serious intent, hidden by the dripping fog of a darkening afternoon while the waters gently smothered memories of burning houses and ballooning black smoke. It was becoming easier not to think about the French families burned alive. Fish or no fish, he would call on the colonel and Vanessa.

The only reminder of the world he had left on the base was the sonorous drone, ominously magnified in the foggy silence, of a V1 flying bomb. It was passing way over, aimed at London, although increasing numbers were falling short in the woods and fields of Kent and Sussex. Some were brought down by Spitfires, though rather more by the bigger and faster Tempests which could fly alongside and tip them off course. Only when the drone had long faded, and the thick white trance was restored, did he pack up his kit and return to his bike by the bridge.

The fog thickened as he approached the village and in following the verge he missed the turning off the lane, realising when he came to an unfamiliar farm entrance. He cycled slowly back, followed by the echoing bark of farm dogs until he came to the gravel of the manor drive.

The only answer to his pull on the bell was a bark, single and muffled. He rang again, surprised by the scale of his disappointment. Although there was nothing he had planned to say and he had no fish to offer, he had come to rely on seeing them both. Even if Vanessa was to become Patrick's, as he feared was inevitable, he would still want to see her. He pulled the bell again, in obstinate refusal to concede.

This time there were footsteps on the drive behind him. Vanessa walked briskly out of the fog, her hands in the pockets of a long gaberdine raincoat. A floppy brown hat covered her ears and hair.

'Hallo, stranger. They been keeping you busy?'

He smiled with relief. 'Could say that, I guess.'

She stood close as she opened the door, which was not locked. 'Time for tea, I hope?'

'Thank-you, ma'am.' She smiled a small smile, like a shared intimacy. He much preferred it to what he thought of as her wider social smile, the one she switched on and off. 'The colonel out?' he continued. He felt disloyal for hoping so.

'Upstairs asleep. He often sleeps in the afternoons. He's not really very well, I'm afraid, as I expect you've noticed.' She crossed the hall, taking off her hat and unbuttoning her coat, leaving him to shut the door. 'I grabbed the chance to go to the post office and stretch my legs.'

He followed her into the kitchen. She filled the kettle, put it on the stove, took a large brown tea-pot from the shelf and said, over her shoulder, 'Could you get cups and saucers from the dresser? Get three, I'll take one up to him.'

They sat at the table while the kettle boiled. The classified ads pages of the local paper were open between them. 'We're thinking of a replacement for Tinker, I'm afraid. He's not got long to go, poor old thing.'

Tinker lay by the stove. He had not got up when they entered, content with lifting his tail and letting it fall.

'Not before he goes, of course. A puppy would probably finish him off. But there are plenty of temptations advertised. Fatal to go and see any before we're ready, though. You can't say no once you see them.'

'What would you get, another spaniel?'

They talked dog breeds while he tortured himself again by imagining her with Patrick. She sat slightly hunched, her hands in her coat pockets folded on her lap, talking naturally and matter-of-factly, while he tried to decide whether this was good because she was relaxed with him or bad because she was indifferent.

She got up to fill the tea-pot. 'You look exhausted,' she said, without looking round. 'Has it been bad?'

Pleased with her attention, he told her about Rouen. He wasn't sure he should – in fact, he was pretty sure he shouldn't – but went on anyway.

'I'm afraid that's the Americans for you,' she said. 'Some of them, anyway. Nice enough individually, very generous, but no night navigation, poor recognition, poor fire discipline, inaccurate bombing. It's not the first time and won't be the last.'

It was strange to hear a woman speak with such authority. 'You know about them, then?'

'I've heard. And met one or two.' She took off her coat and sat again while the tea brewed. She wore a dark jersey and skirt. 'Is it cold in here or is it just me?'

'Seems warm enough to me. You must've got cold while you were out.' There was a pause. 'You've known other pilots, then, not just me and Patrick?'

She nodded, gazing past him at the kitchen sink

and crawled out himself. It was more dangerous then than when we'd gone out the first time because the enemy was thoroughly alerted. I was still in my funk hole, didn't know what to do, hadn't moved an inch, when I heard movement behind me, realised it must be someone from our own lines. Strangely, that did it – I found I could move again. I'd just started to slither round when he found me. We were both lying down, face to face. "You all right?" he whispered.

'"Fine," I said, "I'm sorry."

'He patted me on the helmet. "Don't be."

'"I funked it. Couldn't move. I'm so sorry."

'"Follow me."

'When we got back to our trench I heard him say to Sergeant White, "Concussion. Be OK when he's had a rest. I'll send him back to Battalion HQ with the prisoners, detail two men to go as guards."

'Back in the dugout I tried to explain to Frank again but he cut me short. "Forget it, these things happen. Main thing now is to get the prisoners back quickly so they can get them to Brigade for interrogation. No need to hurry back. That's probably all the action we're getting for the night. Get some sleep somewhere."

'That was the last I saw of him. We delivered the two prisoners after the usual mishaps of trench travel at night, nearly getting shot by our own HQ company sentries. I had a feeling he intended me to stay out of the line and be rested and was perhaps sending a separate message to the CO to that effect, so I didn't hang around to hear it but set off back again with the two guards. Not that I wanted to go back, of course, but I couldn't bear to feel I'd let Frank down. Especially as I'd married Maud.'

'What happened to him?'

'Strange thing about guilt is that you can become possessive about it, hoarding it, treasuring it because it makes you feel special. You, uniquely among all humanity, bear this burden. It's corrosive, like too much grief, turning you inwards on yourself rather than outwards towards others. In the end I had no relief until I told Maud everything. She had known and loved him and if she could forgive me, I reckoned, then I could begin to accept myself. Frank was the love of her life, you see, never me. But I accepted that, too.'

'When was he killed?'

'He was wrong about the rest of the night being quiet. They punished us for the raid with a bout of shelling. The company HQ dugout, where Frank would normally have been, was untouched but he'd remained in the section of trench where we'd come back and it was that corner that was hit. Him and Sergeant White. I got back to find myself in charge of the company. Ironic, eh?'

'So it wasn't your fault? You didn't need to feel too guilty?'

with its high old-fashioned brass taps and the crockery drying on the draining-board. 'There's a lot of air force round here. Lot of Army now, too.'

The thought that she might have had – still have – numbers of pilot boyfriends was fresh torture. There was a call from upstairs. She stood and poured the third cup. 'He's awake. I'll take him his tea. He needs help sometimes.'

Frank stood. 'My I use your bathroom?'

'Follow me.' At the kitchen door she paused. 'It's his heart, you see. There's nothing to be done. He's fine most of the time so long as he takes it easy and has regular rest. But it's aged him and he's often a bit confused when he gets up, more so than normal, so don't mind anything he says.'

He followed her up the stairs, keeping three steps behind for decency's sake. There was a wide landing with four doors opening off and a corridor. She pointed along the corridor. 'Down there.' She knocked on one of the doors and went in, closing it behind her.

It was still closed when he returned to the landing, pausing and listening to her voice. Her tone was soft and encouraging, unlike her usual confident clarity, as if she were talking to a child. One of the other doors was half open, showing what looked like a study with bookshelves and a desk and chair. With a glance at the colonel's door, he stepped in. Beside the desk was a side table with the gramophone on it and, on the lower shelf, a stack of records. Immediately above the desk were four photographs on the wall. One was of a helmeted pilot standing by his Spitfire, another a studio photo of a uniformed flight lieutenant with curly dark hair, broad shoulders and a medal ribbon. The third was the same man in an Aran sweater, sitting on a gate and smiling; the fourth was him in uniform again, posing in a church porch with his bride, Vanessa, on his arm.

'You've penetrated my sanctum.' She was standing in the doorway, her arms folded.

'I'm sorry, I shouldn't have, I just saw the photo of the Spit—'

'It was Johnny's, my husband's. My late husband's.'

'I'm sorry, I didn't—'

'No reason you should.' She came into the room, smiling, and put her hand on his arm. 'It's all right, Frank, don't worry. Not your fault.'

The colonel was on the landing. He was wearing corduroys and his tweed jacket, his hair was tousled and his jacket collar turned up. He pointed down the corridor and said to Frank, 'Just going – won't be a minute.'

Vanessa stepped smartly across to him and straightened his collar. 'We'll be in the kitchen. Come and join us.'

Frank came out onto the landing but the colonel stood staring at him, blinking. 'Got some leave, then?'

'Well, a few hours. No fish, though. Better get back soon.'

The colonel then patted him on the shoulder. 'Good boy, good boy, stick at it. One day at a time, don't think ahead, don't worry how far there is to go, just keep going. That's how you get through.'

'Thank you, sir.'

The colonel headed uncertainly down the corridor. Vanessa touched Frank's arm and he followed her down the stairs. 'See what I mean?' she whispered. 'I don't think he was quite sure who you were. He'll be fine when he comes down and he's a bit more awake.'

'He's persuaded himself he knew my father in the last war. He didn't but he had a friend with the same name. I tried telling him but – well I just let it go now.'

She paused at the foot of the stairs. 'I know, he keeps mentioning it to me. He's getting more and more like that, I'm afraid.' She touched his arm again. 'It's good of you to be so understanding. Thank you, Frank.'

'I'm sorry about your husband.'

She turned her head towards the hall table and moved away. 'He was killed just over a year ago. Over Rouen, funnily enough. His squadron was at Detling. That night you came to dinner, the first time, with those two fish, that was the anniversary of his death. I think the colonel thought it would do us both good to have some company, some distraction, but I just wasn't up to it, I'm afraid. That's why I hid myself away and played those records. They were the numbers Johnny and I used to dance to.'

'I'm so very sorry, if I'd known—'

'You didn't and you shouldn't be.' She looked at him again, this time with the switched-on smile. 'Anyway, if you hadn't come we wouldn't have met, would we?'

'Last time, when you were dancing with Patrick, were they the same records?'

'Some of them. One has to go on. Better pick up your burden and shoulder it than drag it behind you and let it hold you back. I thought it would be good to dance with you both. I hadn't danced with anyone since Johnny.'

He knew what he wanted to say but not how to say it. It came out anyway. 'I didn't realise you wanted me to dance. I thought maybe you and Patrick—'

She shook her head, no longer smiling. 'No, Frank, not another pilot. Patrick's very charming, but no. I know what happens to pilots.'

The colonel came downstairs, looking better, his tread firmer. 'Frank, good to see you. Staying for dinner, I hope?'

'Afraid not, sir. Got to get back. There'll be a

briefing for tomorrow.'

'Come when you can. You're welcome any time, you know that.' He went into the kitchen, leaving them facing each other.

Frank wanted to keep talking. 'I saw lots of French books in your study.'

'All mine. I was brought up partly in France.'

'You speak French, then?'

'We don't have to stand here making conversation. Stay and have some more tea.'

'I love you.'

She said nothing at first, as expressions chased each other like shadows across her face. Then she put her hand on his arm again, shaking her head. 'No, Frank, you can't, you don't know me. You mustn't. I can't return it.'

'I don't mind that. Well, no, I do, but I wanted to say it, wanted you to know.' He put his hand on hers.

'But it means a lot,' she said. 'Thank you for saying it.' She stepped close, brushed his lips with hers and then was gone, walking with hard clear steps across the hall to the kitchen.

Chapter Ten

Again the sky emptied, again Frank was left sweating and trembling, this time with throbbing pains in his temples, wrists and ankles despite his emergency oxygen. It had been sixty seconds – no more – of yanking and heaving on the controls at 25,000 feet and 400 mph. He was panting, his face hot and swollen inside his mask. Worse was the sickening certainty that what he'd just witnessed was no dream brought on by oxygen starvation.

Moments before, the sky had been filled with planes diving, twisting, climbing and turning amidst a firework display of tracer, exploding aircraft and burning bits plunging earthwards. Now it was himself alone apart from, 10,000 feet below, a surviving clutch of ME109s racing for home, blurred shapes against the trees and fields of Normandy.

The scrap took both sides by surprise. The squadron

was returning from a high sweep over the battlefield, in broken cloud and with some mist at ground level. D-Day had come and gone, the Allied armies were ashore but progress had slowed. Day after day they flew sorties aimed at maintaining aerial superiority, but a long period of low cloud had made ground support impossible. Now it had lifted and, through great white chasms in the higher clouds, they glimpsed the battle around Caen where Typhoons, let loose at last, were saving General Patton's bacon by rocketing the advancing German tanks. From that height the Typhoons resembled erratic insects emitting streams of red and white as they incinerated crew after crew of the feared Tiger tanks. The purpose of the sweep was to see off any Luftwaffe fighters who might intervene. Until almost the end, when they were about to turn for home, it was fruitless, conditions making it hard for either side to find their quarry.

But when they emerged from a great bank of cumulus they found themselves flying alongside a flight of nine or ten ME109s. For the briefest of moments it must have looked as if they were all flying home together. Frank was above and behind Patrick and as they came out of the cloud he glanced down to see if there was action on the ground. He should have looked up and about but only half his mind was on what they were doing, the other half in a

149

reverie, lulled by the beat of his Merlin engine. They would probably make it back to the mess in time for lunch and he was thinking yet again of the kaleidoscope of expressions that had flowed across Vanessa's features when he said he loved her. Too fleeting to be individually readable, the impression they left was of surprise, pleasure, sadness and vulnerability, above all vulnerability. He had not seen that in her before.

'Break right now!'

Patrick's voice jolted him but for a second he couldn't get his limbs to move. He had known it in dreams, a paralysing helplessness when trying to flee something, his legs leaden and unresponsive. He would awake in panting panic, feeling he was pressed into the mattress by a great weight. It was like that now; he was willing himself to respond but unable at first even to turn his head. The delay, fractional, unnoticeable to any but him, proved crucial: he lived, Patrick died.

The spell was broken by the shock of yellow tracer feet ahead of his windscreen and the sudden juddering of his plane, shaking him in his seat. He flung the plane up and right. An ME109 that must have been heading straight for him, taking him broadside on, slipped beneath him, tongues of flame leaping through the black smoke pouring from it. Patrick was pursuing it, his cannon lighting up with spurts of flame as he pumped shells into it. Momentarily, way off to his left, Frank glimpsed the Dodger's Spitfire diving away from the fight, straight and true as an arrow. Then the ME109 exploded in a dazzling flash and an enveloping black cloud. Debris flew around Frank, some seemingly suspended in the air. As he banked he saw another plane caught in the explosion, its engine dropping in a ball of fire and one wing – a Spitfire wing, Patrick's wing – see-sawing earthwards.

He could never reconstruct the ensuing seconds. He knew only that he survived them, fighting like an angel. A great black cross on a silvered flank was in front of him. He squeezed his firing button and there were flashes along its fuselage. Then it was gone and he was wheeling left to avoid another Spitfire, then yanking right into a flick roll as an ME109 came at him from below. He tried to catch it before it turned away but as he came out of his roll another came straight at him, head on and firing. He squeezed his firing button again but the plane kept coming, its guns blazing. They were like maddened creatures locked in a duel of self-destruction, each knowing that the first to break off would present the other with a wide and vulnerable target. For an instant the Messerschmitt filled his windscreen and collision seemed inevitable, then it appeared to judder and bits flew off it, then it wasn't there and Frank was hurtling into free sky, his feet and legs tingling and his grip

151

on the controls loosened. He was dizzy and thought he heard someone groan and say something, realising afterwards it could only have been himself. He gripped the controls again and turned back to the fray, but this time the combatants were gone and the sky was empty.

He set course for home knowing that Patrick had died saving him from that ME109. He would have had no chance of getting out of a falling, disintegrating plane, even if he was still alive as the engine and wing dropped away. Frank could have saved himself if he had broken right when Patrick shouted. He knew why he hadn't.

The mood back at base was sombre and febrile. Patrick's death hung heavily over them. As with other deaths, no one spoke about it. There was nothing to say. Instead, they talked about the Dodger's mysterious disappearance. Two others as well as Frank had seen him accelerate away from the fight on a trajectory that would have taken him out over the coast. He had not returned, nor had he rung in from any other airfield where he might have crash-landed. He would have been out of fuel by now. It was after their individual debriefs, when they were in the mess for lunch, that they heard he had broken radio silence by calling up Control with the simple message, 'Am going for a dip. Cancel one late lunch. Out.' That would have been about five minutes, on best estimates, before his fuel ran out. A week or so later a report reached them that a naval minesweeper had reported a distant Spitfire, with no sign of damage, flying evenly and at an acute angle into the sea. The ship investigated but found no wreckage.

Apart from these two losses, there was serious damage to two planes, one of which was written off on landing. Several others, including Frank's, had suffered minor damage. Frank was credited with a kill for the plane he had duelled with head-on and with half a share in a probable, the first Messerschmitt he had fired at. Someone else had also hit it and claimed it went down in flames, but no one else had seen that. The consensus was that each squadron had been as surprised as the other and that neither could claim victory.

No one mentioned Frank's initial delay. They had all been too busy with their own instant reactions, except for Patrick, presumably. Frank said nothing about it himself, though he would not have denied it if anyone had accused him. He almost hoped they would and the more it became clear he had got away with it, the worse he felt. The following day he was summoned by the wing commander.

'Sit down.' The wingco left off signing letters and lit a cigarette, offering Frank one. For all the tiredness etched into his lined face, his manner was never less than brisk. 'Bad business about Patrick. You were friends.'

Frank nodded.

'He always spoke well of you. Well done yesterday, by the way. One and a half is better than anyone else.'

Quite suddenly everything seemed a pretence, everything an effort. He felt he no longer had the energy to pretend. 'Patrick died getting me out of trouble. I was too slow at the start. I didn't react. I—'

The wingco shook his head, exhaling twin jets of smoke through his nostrils. 'That's the way it goes. You'd have done the same for him. Bad business about the Dodger, too. He should've been rested. Time you had a change. That's why I've got you here.'

Frank's heart leapt at the prospect of rest, of not having to go on, of being ordered to stop. 'Thank you, sir, but I don't need a rest. I'm fine, I'm happy to go on.'

'I said a change, not a rest. By which I mean Tempests. There are more Tempests being produced than people who can fly them at the moment. In theory you have to have done a full operational tour before you're let loose on the things. I know you haven't but you're pretty close and they're pretty desperate for experienced pilots. It's a beast to fly but a wonderful weapon when you've mastered it.

We're getting two squadrons here under Bee Beaumont, a good man, so I'm sending you off for Tempest training. You'll enjoy it.' He smiled and picked up his pen. 'Good luck.'

'So the better man died, that's what you're telling me? And it was your fault? Just as with me and your father.'

Frank nodded. They were sitting at the kitchen table. The colonel held his empty pipe, leaning back in his chair, his eyes half-hooded as if he were about to sleep. He had listened to Patrick's account without moving. Now, having spoken, he leaned forward and took his tobacco pouch from his pocket. 'That's the way it goes sometimes. Don't beat yourself up over it. Couldn't be helped.'

'In your case it couldn't, it was just chance that he was shelled where you left him. But in my case it could. It's because I didn't react and the reason I didn't react was that – was that—'

'You funked it.'

'Yes.' It was a relief to say it.

The old man nodded as he filled his pipe. Then he rested it in the ashtray and stood. 'Wait here.'

Frank waited. Vanessa was out for her afternoon walk but if he lingered long enough he would see her. He was to leave for Tempest training in Wiltshire the next day. The colonel reappeared with a long brown leather case, held closed by straps at each end. He stood the other side of the table and held it out to Frank. 'These are yours now.'

Frank stood. 'Well, sir, I don't— what is it?'

'Open it and see.' He lowered it carefully onto the table.

Frank undid the leather straps. Inside, each section neatly slotted into holders, were two split-cane fly rods, beautifully finished and barely used. A label inside the lid announced them as made by Bainbridge of Eton-on-Thames. 'Sir, this is very kind, extremely generous of you but I don't see why – what I've done to deserve them. You must want them for yourself, surely?'

'I want you to have them. Your guilt is a burden you'll have to bear now but pack those rods in your kitbag with it and whenever it gets too heavy take them out and use them. Associate them with it and the guilt will lighten gradually. It will never leave you but it will be bearable.'

'Frank, what a lovely surprise.' The door opened. Vanessa stopped when she saw the rods.

'I've given them to Frank,' said the colonel. 'He'll get more use out of them than I shall now.'

She and the colonel stood looking at each other. 'What a good idea.'

'He's going away for a while. Tempest training.'

'Tempests?' She smiled her social smile at Frank.

'Quite a compliment. But do be careful. They're inclined to run away with you, I believe. More tea.' It was not a question. She emptied the stewed tea from the pot and put the kettle on the stove.

The two men sat. 'Frank was just telling me about Patrick,' the colonel said. 'You remember – his squadron leader who came to dinner.'

'Of course I remember.' She turned to Frank, her hand still on the kettle. 'Hasn't bought it, has he?'

Frank nodded. Again, her use of jargon jarred with him.

'Frank was with him. He was killed by the blast of the plane which was attacking Frank, and which Patrick shot down.'

'He saved me,' said Frank.

'How awful for you.' She let go of the kettle and picked up the kitchen towel, drying her hands as she came over and stood by him.

'It was my fault, I—'

'Frank was a bit slow off the mark, blames himself. I've been telling him he shouldn't.'

She put her hand on Frank's shoulder. 'Of course you shouldn't, you mustn't. If it's anyone's fault it's the Germans'. They started it all.' She squeezed his shoulder. 'I made a fruit cake yesterday. It's in that tin on the dresser. Bit soggy, I'm afraid, but it would be a sin not to eat it. You get it while I do the tea. Plates on the shelf, knife in the drawer.'

They talked about the Tempest. Both seemed to know more about it than he did. 'You're pretty well-informed,' he said. 'I guess your – your – I guess you heard a lot about them.'

'Johnny converted to Tempests just before he was killed,' she said quickly. 'He had one of the early ones. I think each one was more or less a prototype then, they all flew differently. He said it was an acquired taste, you had to work at it, but he grew fond of it, didn't he?'

The colonel, his mouth filled with cake, nodded.

'He went to Wiltshire to convert, too. It'll be good for you to have a break, won't it? Concentrate on flying, not just fighting.'

They talked for another half an hour or so. He felt they were making conversation for his benefit, keeping the ball in the air like a volleyball team at home, with no one saying what needed saying. It was another example of this English disease. Yet he wasn't sure what it was that needed saying. He wanted to continue confessing but there was nothing else to confess. It was plain, anyway, that they wouldn't let him, that they'd brush it aside. He now felt he should never have mentioned Patrick, let alone Johnny. By doing so he had imposed an obligation on them, the obligation of sympathy, that they – she, anyway – had very deliberately not imposed upon him.

'I guess I'd better be getting back.' He stood.

The colonel put down his pipe. 'Come and see us when you're back from Wiltshire.'

'The cake was delicious, really good, thank you.'

She walked into the hall with him. 'Mind what you do with your new toy. Be careful.'

'I'm sorry, I didn't mean to make you talk about Johnny.'

'Don't be. And don't punish yourself over Patrick. We're all human, we just have to manage as best we can.'

'I'll let you know when I'm back.'

'Do.'

He couldn't deal with it, this English politeness. You were never sure quite what was meant, nor how much they meant it. He wanted to kiss her but she was keeping her distance. Yet her gaze was warm, almost affectionate. 'Please do,' she added, as if perceiving his difficulty.

He took her hand and squeezed it. There was a brief answering pressure before she turned away, again leaving him to let himself out. She said something – it might have been, 'I'll look forward to it,' or, 'Be sure you do,' or both. He never discovered which.

Chapter Eleven

In some ways they were easy meat: they flew straight and level, did not turn to avoid attack, did not fire back. In other ways they were difficult, even dangerous: their pulse-jet engines sped them through the skies at 340–370 mph, which meant that – apart from a few up-rated Spitfires and American Mustangs – most fighters could catch and stay with them only by diving, which entailed tricky adjustments. Only the Tempests, capable of 460 mph in level flight, could overhaul the V1 Doodlebugs with ease, choosing their range and moment to fire.

Even now, however, in the new squadron's second week of action against Doodlebugs and Frank's twenty-fifth sortie as a Tempest pilot, it could still be a difficult and sometimes dangerous task. The difficulty was that the prey was not only fast-moving but small, with a wingspan of only sixteen feet and a fuselage only three feet wide. The danger – initially, at least – was that the Tempest's cannon were adjusted for spread-harmonisation, like the pellets of a shotgun, in order to catch a turning fighter or moving train. This meant that to be sure of downing one of these rapid cigar-tubes you had to be close; and sometimes the blast from a ton of high explosive resulted in burned and blackened planes and pilots. When the Tempest wing commander, Bee Beaumont, sought permission to point-harmonise the Tempest cannon so that they focused at three hundred yards, he was refused. He did it anyway.

Now, as Frank closed on another quarry crossing the coast between Eastbourne and Hastings, he knew he could take his time and be sure of a hit, his second that morning. He approached level and from behind until he was about a thousand yards away, then gently descended a hundred feet and closed to three hundred yards. Looking up at the rocket through the Tempest's transparent canopy, he eased up until level again. Once he could feel its wake, he centred his gun-sight on the pulse-jet's exhaust flame and gave it a long burst. The explosion lifted his plane as he turned up and away but with nothing like the force it would have had if he'd been a hundred yards closer.

It was a clear day and the Channel was dotted with ships supporting the invading armies in Normandy. Far off to his left he could make out a flight of Typhoons heading south. As often recently, he was struck by the contrast between the peace of the Downs and the undulating Weald below and what he was doing in his new seven-ton killing machine, which handled – now that he was used to it – with such misleading sweetness.

A red flare shot up from the coast to his right, curving gracefully at the top of its trajectory. He dipped his wing to look inland of it and, sure enough, at about 2000 feet and two miles distant, a small black-bronze cross sped across the green towards London. He wasn't surprised; they were coming over at about a hundred a day now. Flares were another initiative of Bee Beaumont's, signal rockets fired from Royal Observer Corps positions around the coast to indicate V1s to any patrolling Tempests. Frank eased into a long shallow dive, aiming to intersect south of Tonbridge.

He was low on ammunition and, not wanting to risk returning to base unarmed, decided to try what several in the squadron said they'd done. He approached from behind but to one side, out of the rocket's slipstream. He pulled carefully alongside it, close enough to see every detail of its construction but keeping clear of the unwavering flame of the pulse-jet. According to those who'd done it, the trick was to get your wingtip beneath one wing of the flying bomb, then raise it slowly until it disturbed the boundary layer of air around the bomb, causing it to topple away and downwards. You had to do it without any dangerous touching of wings.

Frank descended slightly, increased throttle and edged closer to the Doodlebug until the tip of his right wing was about ten feet beneath the bomb's left. Then, with silent gratitude to the German engineers for making a rocket that flew so straight and true, he began a gentle roll to the left. He knew he was a perfect target for any of the few marauding German fighters still crossing the Channel, but daren't take his eyes off the two closing wings. At first nothing happened but when his wing was a mere two or three feet beneath the other, the Doodlebug lifted its wing and turned almost lazily, but irrevocably, downwards and to its right, flashing its pale blue underside as they parted company. Thereafter it curved in a steepening dive eastwards into the fields and orchards of Kent. With luck, it would make a hole in the ground somewhere, but that was all. Frank pulled up to look around before setting course for home.

It had been a hectic two weeks since his return and it was a few days more before Frank was free to call on the colonel and Vanessa. As well as flying several sorties a day, they had to take on night cover and he hadn't even had time to look up his old squadron, those that remained, anyway. The routine of briefing, standby, flying, debriefing, eating, sleeping and more briefing permitted nothing else, not even writing to his mother. He had managed to get off a letter to her while in Wiltshire and sent the colonel and Vanessa a postcard, after struggling with how to address them. The colonel – Colonel Ovenden – was easy enough, but Vanessa? He realised he didn't even know her surname. He had never asked in what relation she stood to the colonel, assuming at first she was his daughter, then that she was perhaps a niece or something, latterly that she could be his widowed daughter-in-law. Yet there had been no mention of the colonel having a son, and her referring to him as 'the colonel' surely made it unlikely that she was family. A hired help, maybe, to look after him. But she was more familiar than that. Several times he had been on the point of asking but it made him feel clumsy and gauche, particularly as they acted as if it didn't need explaining, as if it was as obvious to him as to them. He couldn't decide whether this was English reticence or English nonchalance, this manner of dealing that was at once inclusive and distancing, making you one of them by assuming nothing needed explaining but at the same time making you feel hopelessly different because you didn't understand.

Eventually, he sent a postcard of a church addressed simply to the manor, saying that he was enjoying his new toy, hoping they were well and that he would see them soon. He included his RAF box number but there was no reply.

One day he had an afternoon free, granted because he was on standby to fly that night between 2330 and 0300. He went over to his old squadron in search of Roddy's bike but couldn't find it and the two pilots he met were new boys who knew nothing of it. He would walk, he decided. There wouldn't be time to fish but it should be walkable provided he didn't linger too long over tea.

The weather continued fine though with some cumulus. Spitfires and Tempests took off and landed throughout his walk, some passing so low that it felt they were buzzing him personally. But these reminders of the world he would shortly return to did not trouble him. The unaccustomed pleasure of walking more than a few yards to the plane, the leafy bounteousness of hedgerows and elms, the ripened cornfields and the anticipation of welcome focused him on the pleasure of this hour, this day, with no thought for the next. Even the thought of Patrick did not, for once, undermine it all. Everything – leaves, colours, shapes of clouds – struck him with heightened particularity.

He smelt it before he saw it, a heavy acrid smell of burnt materials, smoke and dust that lingered on the lane before he stepped into the drive. He noticed brick dust on the hedge and on some holly leaves just before he turned the corner and saw the end wall of the manor, standing alone and intact all the way up to the ridge point where it met the roof, fireplaces and wallpaper looking as if painted on. The rest was rubble, no stairs, no roof, no other walls but a heap of blackened timbers, smashed slates and strewn bricks. The stone steps to the front door were still there, one end of an upturned bath jutted out from a pile of bricks, an undamaged dining chair lay on its side in the drive and the burnt carcass of the Bentley could just be made out beneath the collapsed garage roof. The garden beyond, visible now, was littered with detritus. The greenhouse and potting shed were intact, but with no glass.

'One of them Doodlebugs,' said the woman in the shop. 'Dawn, who lives next door, she was out with her dog and saw it come down, just tipping out of the sky straight onto its nose, not going straight and lower and lower like they usually do. Another five minutes and she'd have been just by the manor and wouldn't be here now. Nor would her dog. Looks like we're out of Senior Service. Just Weights or Woodbines.'

'Woodbines, please. Were they both killed, the colonel and—'

'He was, the old colonel, yes. Wouldn't have known anything about it. And his dog. But Mrs Ovenden was away for the day, thank goodness. She got the early train to London. She was in here the day before, said she was trying to find a job up there. Speaks French, she does, you should hear her, so fast. Fives or tens? We've got twenties in Weights.'

'Tens, please.' They'd be cheaper in the mess but he wanted to keep her talking. 'Mrs Ovenden? I thought she was dead?'

'Old Mrs Ovenden, yes, bless her soul. But I mean young Mrs Ovenden, what lived with him. Vanessa, her name is, was married to his son. Widowed now. Such a lovely boy, he was.'

'Colonel Ovenden had a son, then?'

'Oh yes.' She looked at him, as if he should have known. 'John, his name was. Shot down in France about a year ago. They hadn't been married long. Lovely wedding, it was, the church looked so lovely even in wartime. They invited all the village.'

'When was it, the Doodlebug?'

'This week, a couple of days ago. No – the day before that, Tuesday, when we got some margarine and cheese in. All gone now, needless to say.'

It was the day he had tipped the V1. So had two others, he consoled himself. There was no knowing which. But he couldn't stop. 'What time?'

'In the morning, it was, before we shut for lunch. If it had gone a bit farther it would have been us and the church.'

The time fitted. But one of the others was roughly

then, too. He couldn't remember where, exactly. 'But Vanessa – Mrs Ovenden – is OK? She's still alive?'

'Yes, such a lucky thing. Mind you, a terrible shock to her, coming home to that with nothing but the clothes she stood in. Spent the night at Mary Dobbs's, what used to clean for them. And her losing her husband only last year, that's the family gone now: first old Mrs Ovenden in the Blitz doing voluntary nursing in London, then young John in his plane and now the colonel and I don't think she's much family of her own, to speak of. Didn't even have time to have a baby. Will that be all? Any matches?'

'No, thanks, I use a lighter. Where is she now, still with Mary Dobbs?'

The woman took his money and rang the till, counting out his change slowly. 'Went back to London the next day – no, day after, it must have been. The day the bread should have come and didn't. She said she had a friend in London she could stay with, the one what's helping her find a job. Don't suppose we'll be seeing much more of her down here, no reason for her to come any more, not even a roof over her head. Poor thing. She was a nice lady, always so polite.'

'Did she leave a forwarding address?'

'Her friend's, yes, Mary or me will send anything on. And some solicitors in Tonbridge, the colonel's solicitors, she said. She left their address too, in case anything happens to her.'

'May I have it?' The woman looked at him. 'Hers, I mean. I knew them both, you see, I used to call on them pretty regular. I'd like to write to her.'

The woman's grey-green eyes, enlarged by her glasses, remained on his. 'Not a friend of John's though, were you? Didn't serve with him?'

He nodded. 'Different squadrons.'

She paused long enough for him to fear she was going to refuse but then she bent and sorted through some papers beneath the counter. 'Here it is but you can't keep it; you'll have to copy it out.'

It was an address in Pimlico, a part of London he hadn't heard of. 'Is there a telephone number?'

She shook her head. 'Quicker to write, time it takes people to get through to London from here. Cheaper, too. I did give you your change, didn't I?'

He wrote that night, before standby, but it was a fortnight before he had a reply. Those two weeks were the most intense period of the V1 bombardment, which ended when the Allied armies overran the launch sites. Each time Frank shot one down or flipped one, he thought of the manor. He still didn't know whether it was his first flipper that had hit it or the one flipped by someone else at about the same time, or simply a rocket that had fallen short as they sometimes did. It might have been possible to narrow the options, given time he didn't have, but he preferred not to know. The colonel, meanwhile, occupied almost as much of his mind as Vanessa, in an intermittent interior dialogue in which the colonel's walnut voice was ever present. He didn't miss him because it was as if he was still there.

Vanessa's reply coincided with the temporary withdrawal of the squadron's Tempests for improvements and re-adaptation to the roles they were designed for, fighter escort and long-range intruder. There was also a shortage of spares because of strikes at factories in Preston. It meant he at last had some leave.

Her reply was brief but encouraging. She was pleased to hear from him, had not known how to get in touch, was doing war work while camping in her friend Margaret's flat, suggested they met in Lyons Corner House opposite Charing Cross station. She had no phone but if he wrote with a date, giving a few days' notice, she could probably do it. What had happened was a great shock and sadness.

They met on a wet Thursday. His train was late because the V2 rockets had begun to bombard London. Unlike the V1s, they fell without warning and couldn't be shot down or deflected. One had exploded in Woolwich that morning, killing dozens of munitions girls. More were anticipated and the trains reverted to air-raid drill, creeping along the track at 5–10 mph so that drivers had time to spot broken or missing rails. The V2s were much feared.

Frank pushed his way through the crowd outside Charing Cross station without noticing Nelson's column to his left. He was unused to crowds and the press of people made the solitude of his cockpit in the sky almost more attractive than frightening. The Corner House was thronged with uniforms, mainly Army, and the noise was oppressive. Every table was taken and the spaces between were cluttered with kitbags, gas masks, greatcoats and helmets. He could see no other officers. A pair of Redcaps – military police who patrolled every major station – eyed diners through the windows from the Strand.

He waited inside the door, where he had thought she would be. Perhaps she was late as well. It was too hot, too thick with smoke, too crowded, they wouldn't be able to hear themselves speak. He would suggest somewhere else when she came. Then he saw her wave from a table by one of the Strand windows. Suffused with relief, he couldn't help smiling as he squeezed his way over to her. She wore a tightly belted fawn raincoat with a matching hat, her hair tied in a bun. The table was for two, with two teas and two buns.

'I'm sorry, the tea's cold and there's only a bun because I had to order something without knowing what you'd want in order to be allowed to keep the place. I should have realised how crowded it would be at lunchtime. I've only twenty minutes left, I'm afraid. Tell me everything, what you're doing, how you are. I'm so pleased we could meet.'

He didn't mind anything as long as she was there. He drank his cold tea and ate the stale buttered bun without noticing. She smiled all the time, as he did. Her crooked teeth were attractive to him now, whiter than most people's. The smiling stopped when he mentioned the colonel.

'At least it was quick,' he said.

'That's what we always say. We have to, I suppose.'

She looked through the window at the crowd outside the station. He felt he had blundered, reminding her of her husband. 'He wouldn't have known anything about it.'

She shrugged and looked back at him. 'He was very fond of you.'

'I didn't realise that Johnny was his son, that you were his daughter-in-law.'

'Did you not? Really?'

'He never mentioned him. Nobody did until I saw those photos.'

'But the fishing rods he gave you, those were Johnny's. Did you not realise?'

'How could I? No one said anything. I wouldn't have accepted them.' He had raised his voice and

172

perhaps sounded annoyed, but couldn't help it. 'Is it an English thing, not mentioning people when they're dead? It's the same on the squadron but it's more understandable there because you've got to go on.'

'So has everyone. It's the same for all of us.' She spoke quietly.

'He said, "They're yours now," like he was anointing me, making me his son.'

'Yes.'

'But I didn't even know.'

'That was the point. He didn't want to burden you with the obligation of sympathy. He wanted to spare you that. He probably thought you had enough on your plate.'

'He told me all about how the other Frank Foucham, the one he kept thinking was my father was killed in the last war as a result of saving him. Just like with me and Patrick.'

'That may have been deliberate, too, despite his confusion.'

It was not going as he'd wanted. He felt exasperated and at the same time that he was being unreasonable. The smiling intimacy of the first few minutes had evaporated and there was a distance between them now. He held up his hands. 'I'm sorry, I didn't mean it to be like this.'

'It's quite all right, Frank.'

That made it worse, that impossible-to-read social

tone again. 'Another thing, I – that V1 that hit the manor. It might have been mine, might have been me that tipped it. Maybe that was my fault too.'

She reached across the table and took his hand. 'No, Frank, not you, don't blame everything on yourself. It's the Germans' fault, Hitler's fault, it's not you. Stop thinking about yourself.' She let go. 'Now, I have to go. I have to be back at my office by two. Will you walk with me?'

It was a quaint way to put it but he could have wept with relief. He had thought she was about to leave him and that that would be it, no more talk. They had a brief, good-natured argument about the bill, which she let him win, and then walked down Whitehall to the War Office where she worked. 'What do you do there?'

'I'm afraid I can't say.' She smiled. 'I'm not just being mysterious. I'm not allowed to talk about it. But it's nothing like as exciting or important as what you're doing, I promise.'

Walking in uniform along Whitehall proved a minefield strewn with military top brass. He found himself saluting every ten yards and she soon started to laugh. She slowed as they approached the War Office. 'You'd better not come to the door or they'll think you're official.'

'I am official, just not officially with you.' They stopped. 'May I see you again?'

'Of course.'

It was awkward. Standing on the pavement outside the War Office in uniform, he couldn't touch or kiss her as he wanted. 'It's – I – I can't say what I'd like to say, here. I'm sorry.'

Her expression was solemn, which made him feel more awkward. 'What time do you have to be back?'

'No time. I'm on leave.'

'Come to my flat at six-thirty. You have the address.'

Chapter Twelve

It was a basement flat in one of Pimlico's stucco-fronted nineteenth-century streets. Frank had spent the afternoon wandering around central London, looking for famous sights but recognising only Big Ben and Buckingham Palace. The rest, though busy, was tired, drab and colourless apart from the willow herb that colonised the bomb sites and the uniformed servicemen of various nationalities without whom no street scene seemed complete. The civilians looked pale, preoccupied and indifferent.

Later, he took himself to a cinema in Leicester Square and watched a film about eighteenth-century pirates, smoking four cigarettes and paying attention only when Pathé news came on with scenes of jubilant French civilians greeting Allied forces in Europe and reports of heavy fighting in Holland. Most of the time he fantasised about what was going to happen in her flat but without being able to imagine anything convincing, or even specific.

The flat was small and shabbily furnished but the dim yellow light bulbs and the smell of cooking lent it the illusion of homeliness. She wore a dark skirt and white blouse and began apologising before he was properly through the door. 'Margaret's away in Portsmouth yet again – she works for the Navy and is up and down like a yo-yo – and since I arrived there hasn't been time to sort anything out, hence the mess, I'm afraid. It's also damp – can you smell it? – but the landlady lives in Worcester and isn't interested so long as she gets her rent. Dinner will be pretty awful, too – just a morsel of ancient mince and even older potatoes with, if they haven't rotted, some runner beans I brought up from Kent. Rationing bites – if that's the word – harder in London than elsewhere.' She laughed. 'And no wine or beer. Well, there is a bottle of red in the kitchen but it's Margaret's and I think she's saving it for some special occasion like the end of the war or marrying her admiral.'

'I should have got one. I saw a – an off-licence, is that what they're called? It was quite near, I'll go back and—'

'No you won't, it won't be open yet and anything they've got is bound to be hideously expensive and bad. That's if they've got it at all. We'll make do with tea. There's masses of that because Margaret doesn't drink it so she just saves up her rations and gives it away.'

'I didn't know anyone in England didn't drink tea.'

'You don't know the English yet.' She smiled. 'You can put your cap and gas mask down, you know, we're not about to be inspected.'

The kitchen was a narrow galley with barely enough room for two. Beyond it was an equally narrow bathroom that felt and smelt damp. There was one bedroom – Margaret's – which he didn't see. Vanessa cooked on an oven with two gas rings, both of which were feeble. 'Pressure must be down,' she said. 'This may take some time.'

They ate at the table in the living room. 'Where do you sleep?' he asked.

'There.' She nodded at the sofa. 'It unfolds into a bed. It's not bad, quite comfortable. I thought about using Margaret's, which is a proper double, but I don't think we should. I couldn't relax.' She smiled. 'If you want to stay, that is.'

He looked at her. 'I thought you – no more pilots, you said—'

'I know. And I meant it when I said it. And it's no good falling in love with me, I still mean that. But—'

'You think I need it? You're taking pity on me?'

'Doing my bit for the war effort.' Her eyes were still smiling. 'But only if you really want to.'

178

Frank felt suddenly nervous, almost like a take-off, but he smiled. 'I do want to, I really do.'

Later, in the early hours, he lay awake while she dozed. It was done; he was qualified, part of wider mankind at last. But he didn't feel any different. There was none of the euphoria he had felt on getting his wings or completing his Spitfire training. Only this woman by his side who had accepted him, generously, mysteriously. He sensed already that he might never really know why, but he was grateful.

At about three o'clock they got up and made tea. She showed him how. 'It's so important to warm the pot first, then one spoonful for each drinker and one for the pot. Then you must – must – let it make.'

'Let it make?'

'Leave it to stew for a few minutes.' She held up her hand. 'Mind – careful with the kettle, it's spitting boiling water.' They were both naked.

'I'm learning a lot tonight.'

She kissed his neck. 'You're learning fast.'

'Did you know I'd never—'

'I guessed.'

Breakfast was more tea accompanied by stale bread toasted under the grill. 'Only margarine, I'm afraid,' she said. 'Nothing else here. You live better in your mess.'

They talked about practicalities – what would become of the ruined manor, the colonel's will, her prospect of another job in the War Office which would make greater use of her French. He walked back to Whitehall with her in a thin rain, the pavements teeming with people doing the same. Big Ben was showing ten to nine as they crossed Parliament Square. He slowed. 'Thank you for doing your bit for the war effort.' He wanted to say more but didn't know how to put it. It was easier, less embarrassing, to affect an off-handedness which she would recognise as affected, therefore not meant. He must be catching the English disease, he thought, playing the English game.

'It was my pleasure too, you know.'

'May I come up and see you again?'

'I hope you will.'

'Even though I'm a pilot?'

'Especially.' She stopped, raised her hand to his cheek and kissed him briefly on the lips. 'Goodbye, Frank.'

He levelled off at 150 feet, having just led his flight of three in a wide descending turn away from the train. They had spotted it through a gap in the cloud and, with luck, it might not realise it had been seen. Even if it had, their leisurely turn out of sight from 10,000 feet might tempt it to assume the marauding Tempests had other business. But such trains were very much their business. Briefed primarily to sweep for German fighters, they had been told that targets of opportunity such as goods trains were just as important, especially trains such as this with mysterious long canvas-covered loads that might be rockets or rocket parts. There were anti-aircraft guns mounted on every other truck.

He called to his flight, 'Going down in ten seconds,' and led them on a gentle descent through the cloud until they came out over flat, featureless heathland. Since his unexpected promotion to flight lieutenant, every mission seemed busier. Having to think of and for others left no time for daydreaming nor even for his old familiar, his fear. It was still there but feeling it, indulging it, had become a luxury he no longer had time for. Reckoning they must be six or seven miles from the train, he called out, 'Target ahead. Going down. Form echelon to starboard behind me.' He tightened his harness straps, lowered his seat a notch for gunsight vision and switched on the sight. He would take the engine end, which had the most flak, and force the German gunners to divide their fire to cover them all.

Very soon the train was in sight, still some miles ahead. It was a long one, almost the length of the embankment and going very slowly from right to left ahead of them, suggesting it was prepared for attack. They had to go for it now or not at all. Frank no longer hesitated over anything. After a quick check that the others were lined up behind, he opened up to 450 mph and took his Tempest down to 50 feet, almost level with the train. As soon as he was in range he pressed the firing button. His cannon shells kicked up stones and sparks from the railway, then, gratifyingly, spurts of flame and jets of steam from the engine itself. At the same time the ack-ack lit up, blinding white flashes running the length of the train. For an instant, no more, Frank saw again the flash of sunlight on the colonel's river.

THE END

POSTSCRIPT

This story of friendship through fishing is an imagined elaboration of a real incident described by Pierre Clostermann in his memoir, *The Big Show*. Clostermann was a Frenchman who flew with the RAF during the Second World War, becoming one of the RAF's top-scoring fighter aces and eventually France's most highly decorated citizen. His book is an outstanding account of aerial warfare and should be read by anyone with an interest in that war.

I have drawn on it and on other accounts by pilots of the period for my attempted evocation of what it was like to fly and fight in those planes. Naturally, any errors or lapses are entirely my doing. The characters of the colonel, Vanessa and Frank Foucham himself are imaginary, though the story of the other Frank Foucham's courtship and the woman he wanted to marry originates within my own family.

Read on for an exclusive extract
from Alan Judd's new novel,

DEEP
BLUE

Coming from Simon & Schuster in January 2017

Chapter One

The Present

Agent files – paper files, anyway – told stories. It was never quite the whole story – nothing was ever that – and they could be misleading, repetitive and elliptical, but as you opened the buff covers and fingered the flimsy pages of carbon-copied letters and contact notes, and the thicker pages of Head Office minutes or telegrams from MI6 stations, a skeleton became a body and eventually a person. It was the story of a relationship; sometimes, almost, of a life. And sometimes, as with the file that Charles Thoroughgood sat hunched over that evening, it bore the ghostly impress of another story, an expurgated presence that had shaped the present one without ever being mentioned.

Files rarely lied in terms of content; their lies were usually by omission, nearly always on security grounds. In this case Charles knew those grounds well, having written much of what was in the file, and nearly all of what wasn't, many years before.

Pellets of rain splattered against his office window, invisible behind the blinds he had insisted upon despite assurances that the security glass could not be seen through. Having spent much of his operational career penetrating the allegedly impenetrable, he was reluctant to accept blanket security assurances. The more confident the assertion, the less he trusted it, and now, as Chief of MI6, he was better able to assert his prejudices than at any point in his eccentric and unpredictable ascent to the top. But not as much as he would have liked; Head Office was still in Croydon and the government seemed in no hurry to fulfil its promise of a return to Whitehall.

He was on volume three of the file, the final volume, reading more slowly as he neared the point where he had joined the case as a young officer on the Paris station during the Cold War. He was alone in the office but for the guards and a few late-stayers, having sent his private secretary home. Sarah, his wife, was also working late, the common fate of City lawyers. The file was a relief from his screen with its unending emails and spreadsheets; also an escape into a world which, because it was past, seemed now so much simpler and clearer than the present. But it had seemed neither simple nor clear then.

There was no hint of a link to another file, no reference to papers removed. When at last he found what he sought he moved the green-shaded desk lamp closer and sat back in his chair, the file on his lap. Movement reactivated the overhead lights, which he disliked for their harshness, but if he stayed still for long enough they would go out. The desk lamp he had brought in himself, against the rules.

The paper he sought was in two sections, the first typed in Russian in Cyrillic script, the second a translation into English by someone from the Russian desk in Century House, the old Head Office during much of the Cold War. They should not have been in this file at all, an ordinary numbered P file belonging to a dead access agent run by the Paris station. Josef, as Charles had known him, was a Russian émigré who, unusually, had been allowed out of the Soviet Union on marrying a secretary from the French embassy. Before that he was a journalist who had committed some minor indiscretion which had earned him ten years in a labour camp, in the days when ten years was what you got for being available to fill a quota, especially if you were Jewish. Settled in France, he had come to the notice of the Paris station, which had recruited him to get alongside visiting Russians. The relationship with the Secret Intelligence Service lasted many years, sustained by snippets from Josef which usually promised more than they delivered, and by payments from SIS, before Charles was sent to terminate him. That was when the case became interesting.

The paper did not, in fact, pertain to Josef at all, though that would not have been apparent to anyone reading the file. It was recorded that Josef had been in a labour camp, so a first-person account of a visit to the camp years after it had closed would be assumed to be his. The account had been left on Josef's file after other papers had been silently removed, doubtless because whoever weeded the file had made the same mistaken assumption. By the time Charles had discovered it both Josef and Badger, code-name of the author of the paper, were dead. It might have drawn attention to the Badger case to have transferred papers to it years later. Not that anyone read old paper files any more. Charles was probably the only person still serving who knew both cases.

There was no real need for him to re-read Badger's account of his visit to his former prison camp. Charles remembered it well enough and his renewed interest in the case now, so many years later, was not because of that. He read it partly because he was nostalgic, partly to revive his sense of the man known as Badger, whose own file he had yet to re-read, and partly in penance, acknowledgement of unfulfilled promise. The description of the camp visit was intended by Badger to be part of the memoir he never wrote, an indication of what he hoped to publish when safely resettled in the West. But he never was resettled and this was the only chapter written. Charles had promised that, if anything happened to Badger, he would see it published somewhere. And never had.

Turning to the typewritten English translation, marked by Tippexed alterations and the translator's margin comments in pencil, Charles read:

Since I was in that remote region, the region of my last camp, and with time to spare before the flight back to Moscow, I told my driver to take me to it. He was puzzled. 'There's nothing there, it was closed years ago. Just the huts and the wire and some of the old guards who have nowhere else to go.'

'Take me.'

It was farther from the airport than I thought and there was fresh snow, unmarked by other car tracks. It was fortunate that the driver knew the way because I should never have found it, hidden in a clearing in the midst of the forest. The iron gates were open and, judging by the depth of snow piled up against them, had been so since autumn. The grey sky was breeding more snow now and on either side the high outer fence stretched into the blurred distance, sagging in places. The watchtowers stood like tall black cranes, one of them with a dangerous list. Inside the wire the huts were squat white shapes with here and there a misshapen one where the roof had collapsed. The doors at the ends, shielded by overhangs, were mostly shut but some sagged open on rotted hinges.

I told my driver to wait and keep the engine and heater running. Then I walked slowly through the gates. There were other footprints in the snow leading to the first hut, a larger H-shaped one which used to be the guardroom. Behind it was the inner fence with another set of open gates. Within that fence were the huts. The guardroom door opened before I reached it. I wasn't surprised. The sight of a shiny black ZiL and an official in a long black overcoat with a sable astrakhan and matching gloves was not a common one for the wretches within. A hunched figure hobbled out, muffled in old clothes and using a stick. He hurried over as if afraid to miss me.

'Greetings, greetings, I am Kholopov, Ivanovich Kholopov. I was sergeant here. I am your guide, if you wish.'

He had a thin dirty face and his lips were never still, working continuously. He looked smelly. I knew he would be, I knew exactly how he would smell, but I had no need to get that close.

'I know the camp well, I know everything about it, I have been here nearly thirty years. I worked here, I was sergeant of the guards.'

I took off one glove and fished out a few coins from my coat pocket. I didn't bother to count them. He held out his hand, his glove worn through on the palm, and I dropped them into it without touching him.

'Thank you, thank you kindly. What would you like to see – the kitchen, the offices, the punishment cells, the graveyard, the huts, the bathhouse? It is all empty, all available.'

'Everything. Show me everything.'

That puzzled him. 'Of course, of course, I can

show you every hut, every bunk. Only there are very many and it will take time—'

'I will tell you when to stop.' I noticed now that he had a twitch in his left cheek.

'With pleasure, it is pleasure. Please follow me.'

We crunched through the snow together, slowly because of the curious way he hobbled. He told me about the building of the camp in the 1930s, initially by the first prisoners sent to it who lived – and often died – in holes in the ground until the huts were up. He described its expansion, then its gradual contraction after the death of Stalin until its closure in the Gorbachev era, by which time it housed only a few politicals, as he called us.

'But when Comrade Gorbachev let the prisoners go the authorities forgot about us, the guards and administrators. We stayed, we had nowhere to go. How can we go anywhere? Where could we go? There is no work for us here but we cannot afford to move. Unless they open the camp again.' His laugh became a prolonged cough. 'We have pensions but they are a pittance, which is why we have to beg from generous visitors such as yourself.'

We reached the first of the huts inside the inner wire. The number one was still just visible in faded white on the wooden door. 'We can go in if you want but there is nothing there, nothing to see. They're all the same. In this block there are numbers one to thirty-nine, the rest are in the other block.

Twenty prisoners to a hut but sometimes there were more. They are all the same, the huts. So were the prisoners. Over there are the camp offices and the punishment cells and the bathhouse and the sick bay and our own quarters. They are more interesting. These are just huts.'

I offered him a cigarette. He glanced as if to check that he had not misunderstood, then grabbed one. 'Thank you, thank you.' His eyes lingered on the packet, which he couldn't read because they were American, Peter Stuyvesant. His eyes lingered too on my gold lighter. 'Number thirty-seven,' I said. 'Take me to thirty-seven.'

The cigarette seemed to give him energy and his lop-sided hobble through the rows became more rapid. The smoke was good and pungent in the cold air.

'You see, they are all the same,' he said again when we reached it.

'Open it.'

I sensed he was reluctant, probably because of the effort involved. He put his cigarette between his lips, leaned his stick against the wall, pushed down on the handle and put his shoulder to the door. It was obviously stiff at first but then opened so freely that he nearly lost his balance. He stood back so that I could look in. 'Nothing to see, just the bunks. They're all the same.'

He had to move as I stepped in. It took a while for my eyes to adjust to the gloom. There were sprinklings of snow on the earth floor beneath the closed wooden window-hatches. The ceiling was low, the wooden double bunks lined the sides, some with broken slats, others still with remnants of old straw. The gangway down the middle was too narrow for two to walk side by side and to get between the bunks you had to go sideways. There was an old metal bucket on the floor by the door and a musty smell. It felt colder inside than out.

I walked two-thirds of the way down and stopped by the lower bunk on the left side. It was no different to all the others, of course. My guide hobbled behind me.

'You knew someone who was here?' he asked.

I didn't answer. After another minute or so of fruitless and circular contemplation, I turned back up the aisle. You live with the past but you can't live it. I left my guide struggling to close the door and headed back towards the gates. The snow was thicker now and the outlines of distant huts rapidly became indistinct. Eventually I heard him shuffling and panting and he caught up with me.

'Is there anything else – the punishment cells, the camp offices?'

I was between the inner and outer fences, approaching the H-shaped guardroom, when he made one last effort, pointing with his stick. 'I could show you the cookhouse. We use it. It still has the ovens and pots and pans—'

That made me stop and think. 'No,' I said. 'That was the guards' cookhouse. The cookhouse for the prisoners was that one, there.' I pointed at a long low building just inside the inner fence.

He followed my gaze, then looked back at me, his lips still for once. 'You are right. I had forgotten. I have been here too long, I am too familiar. But you, how could you—'

'I was here.'

We stared at each other in a long silence, but for the hiss of the snow. Those three words, three simple words, sunk into him like stones in a pool. Who were the prisoners, the real prisoners? And how could I be a senior official with a ZiL and furs? I took the cigarettes and the remaining coins from my pocket. He dropped his stick in the snow and held out his cupped hands. He was still staring, uncomprehending, as my car pulled away.

At the foot of the original Russian text was a hand-written note in English, in Badger's characteristic forward-sloping hand and his usual brown ink: *So you see, Charles, we are all prisoners really, even the guards. Tell your people who doubt my motivation – is this not enough?*

Charles closed that volume of Josef's file and put it with its mate. Then he picked up Badger's file, a slim single volume also buff-coloured but this time with a red stripe, a different number system and a white stick-on label with heavy black lettering saying, 'Closed. Do not digitise.' He had stuck that on himself years before, proof of rare premonition. It meant the case had remained secret and, unlike digitised files, was fully recoverable.

Alan Judd
Inside Enemy

From the author of *Legacy*, now a major BBC Film, comes a brilliant new novel for fans of le Carré, Graham Greene and Charles Cumming.

Charles Thoroughgood is now the recently-appointed chief of a reconstituted MI6, tasked with halting the increasingly disruptive cyber attacks on Britain, which are threatening government itself and all the normal transactions of daily life – not to mention a missing nuclear missile-carrying submarine.

The murder of one of Thoroughgood's former agents and the escape from prison of a former colleague turned traitor, whom Charles helped convict, brings danger on all sides.

Thoroughgood ploughs a lonely furrow in Whitehall in his belief that all these elements are connected, a theory which dramatically gains credibility when his wife, Sarah, disappears . . .

Alan Judd
Uncommon Enemy

From a prison cell, in which he has been held on
suspicion of breaking the Official Secrets Act,
Charles Thoroughgood awaits not only his bail,
but also the reappearance of the woman whom
all the major roads in his life have led back to.

After his years in the army and then with MI6,
Charles has begun a new chapter in his life with
the Secret Intelligence Agency, shadowing the
movements of a suspected double agent.

Charles knows that he has nothing to hide, and as
he casts his mind over the course of recent events,
he begins to suspect a more sinister motivation, both
personally and politically, behind his incarceration . . .